THE SHADE OF SANTA FE

THE MYSTERY HOUSE SERIES, BOOK SEVEN

Eva Pohler

Eva Pohler Books
20011 Park Ranch
San Antonio, Texas 78259
www.evapohler.com

Publisher's Note: This is a work of fiction. Names, characters, places, and incidents are a product of the author's imagination. Locales and public names are sometimes used for atmospheric purposes. Any resemblance to actual people, living or dead, or to businesses, companies, events, institutions, or locales is completely coincidental.

Book Layout ©2017 BookDesignTemplates.com

Book Cover Design by Keri Knutson and B Rose DesignZ

The Shade of Santa Fe/ Eva Pohler. -- 1st ed.
Paperback ISBN: 978-1-958390-30-6

Contents

For all Asian Americans who were detained in prison camps in America during World War II and their families.

CHAPTER ONE

Palo Duro Canyon

W hen was the last time we did a road trip together?" Ellen wondered from behind the wheel of the rental car.

Tanya, who sat in the front passenger's seat, was twisting her blonde hair into a messy ponytail on top of her head. "Wasn't it when we took our kids to Colorado?"

"Was it really that long ago?" Sue said from the backseat. "Heck, Lexi was in the ninth grade when we did that."

Ellen glanced at Sue in the rearview mirror. "That can't be right, can it?"

"It's been the train or the plane ever since," Sue said, her brown eyes confident.

"Every time I fly," Tanya began, "I'm reminded of why I hate flying. But now that we've been on the road for two days, I'm reminded of why I hate *driving*."

"You mean *riding*," Sue said from the back.

Ellen laughed. "And *sleeping*."

"I haven't slept a wink since we left Sweetwater," Tanya said with a defensive tone.

"Well, I don't think it was Ellen I heard snoring," Sue said. "At least, I hope it wasn't."

Tanya turned to face Sue. "You laugh all you want. I wasn't the one who left a line of toilet paper from the bathroom to my bedroom last night."

Ellen giggled. "That was pretty funny. You still haven't explained how that happened, Sue."

"You don't want to know," Sue said.

"I started to roll it up this morning," Tanya said, "but when I saw that it continued beneath Sue's door, I was afraid of what might be on the end of it."

"Oh, stop!" Sue cried, laughing at herself.

"Sounds like an episode of *If That House Could Talk*," Ellen said, still laughing.

"I'm sure more interesting things have happened in that old bed and breakfast in Sweetwater," Sue insisted.

"Oh, look!" Ellen pointed. "There it is."

After hours of driving on a flat, uninteresting landscape, Ellen was delighted to see the Grand Canyon of Texas, Palo Duro Canyon, come into view with all its glorious reds, pinks, and purples.

"It's beautiful," Tanya said.

"It's lovely to look at," Sue began, "but you still aren't getting me to go hiking tomorrow. Your chances of seeing a unicorn are greater."

"We're just asking you to keep an open mind," Tanya said.

Sue sighed. "If you want to get rid of me, just say so. No need to hide my body at the bottom of a canyon."

"There's a very easy trail from the cabin we're staying at," Ellen said. "Alison could walk it when she was three."

"You still haven't told us why you brought *us* instead of Brian," Sue said, deflecting.

Ellen frowned at Sue in the rearview mirror. "Does there have to be a reason for wanting to go on a trip with my friends?"

"You're technically still newlyweds." Sue tucked a strand of brown hair behind one ear. "Is there trouble in paradise?"

"Brian's not interested in shopping in Santa Fe," Ellen said. "I thought it was something we girls would enjoy more."

Tanya gave her a sideways glance. "Brian loves to shop. It sounds like he loves to do everything with you."

"Maybe that's the problem," Sue speculated. "Is Brian smothering you, Ellen?"

Ellen parked in front of their cabin. It was made of stone and built into the canyon rim. She and Paul had come with the kids on two different road trips when the kids were little.

"He's just so different from Paul," Ellen said. "Paul and I spent as much time apart as we did together."

They climbed from the vehicle and carried their luggage to the rustic cabin. The panoramic views beneath the afternoon sun boasted rock formations that glistened like diamonds and uplifted Ellen's spirit as she unlocked the door and pushed it open for her friends.

Tanya entered first. "It has a fireplace?"

"Two, actually," Ellen said. "One in each bedroom."

"Unfortunately, it's hotter than a firecracker," Sue said. "That would have been a nice feature in winter."

"At least it has air conditioning," Tanya said.

"The musical only runs in the summers," Ellen pointed out. "Speaking of which, we better hurry if we want to get our meal before the show starts."

The natural amphitheater built into the canyon wall was bigger than Ellen had remembered, as was the crowd of people in line for the chuckwagon steak, baked potato, and corn-on-the-cob dinner. To fight the summer heat, misters kept the air cool around the covered picnic tables. On the opposite side of the path were vendors with jewelry, textiles, and art for sale.

Once they had their plates and were seated at one of the tables, Tanya asked, "How long did you say the show lasts?"

"Two hours, I think," Ellen said. "Don't worry. You'll love every minute of it. They do an incredible job."

"This food is delicious," Sue said with lifted brows. "I wasn't expecting it to be so good."

"There's peach cobbler for dessert, so save room," Ellen said.

"What made you choose to bring us *here* and to Santa Fe?" Sue asked. "You've already seen the show, and although you *said* you wanted to shop for turquoise, you don't really wear that much jewelry."

"Not just the turquoise," Ellen said. "The art. Santa Fe is an artist's buffet."

"I think there's more to it than that," Sue said.

"What are you? Psychic?" Ellen asked.

Sue shrugged. "I've told you many times that I have the gift."

"Speaking of psychics," Tanya said, "I saw one over by the jewelry. We should ask for a reading before the show. If Ellen won't tell us why we're here, maybe that psychic will."

Ellen sighed. "Okay, okay. I found a house I might want to buy in Santa Fe."

"What?" Sue and Tanya said at the same time.

"I want an artist's retreat," Ellen explained. "And where better than in Santa Fe?"

"But you have an art studio in your back yard," Tanya pointed out.

"Well, it's turned into a woodworking shop, too," Ellen said.

Sue grinned. "That's cute. I can imagine you in there with your paint brushes while Brian works on his wood."

Tanya giggled. "That sounded nasty."

Sue laughed while Ellen glanced around at the others nearby, hoping no one had overheard.

"You don't like sharing, I guess," Tanya said.

Ellen tilted her head to the side. "He uses power tools. It's not the retreat it once was."

Sue and Tanya lifted their brows.

"I have absolutely no regrets about marrying him," Ellen said. "I love him. I really do. But we're still adjusting. I'm still adjusting and adapting to my new normal, you know?"

Tears welled in Ellen's eyes. It had been harder than she'd anticipated to make a new life with a new man. She'd been used to the way she and Paul had fit together. It had been comfortable. As exciting as it was to be in love with Brian, it was also exhausting. She needed her space.

"I get it," Tanya said. "No worries."

"I'm sure you'll find your footing soon," Sue added.

Tanya took a sip of her iced tea. "So, tell us about the property you want to buy."

Ellen leaned forward. "It's a three-bedroom, two-bath, 1600 square-foot home on the side of a hill with views of the mountains. I like the modern architecture—simple, with lots of windows. And it's only a five-minute drive from the plaza."

"Sounds nice," Sue said. "When do we get to see it?"

"I have an appointment with the realtor on Friday morning," Ellen said.

"What's today?" Sue asked. "Wednesday?"

"Yes, Wednesday," Ellen said before taking a bite from the fresh, buttery cob of corn.

"It's not haunted, is it?" Tanya asked of the house.

"I don't think so," Ellen said. "But it's been vacant for quite some time."

Sue arched a brow. "Interesting."

Since they had plenty of time before the show, they browsed the vendor tables after they'd finished their meal. As promised, Tanya stopped at the table belonging to the psychic and asked for a reading.

The psychic took her hand and frowned.

"What's wrong?" Tanya glanced nervously at Sue and Ellen before turning back to the psychic. "Do you sense something bad?"

"Are you ladies traveling to Santa Fe?" the psychic, who looked to be in her mid-forties, asked. She had vibrant red hair pulled up into a tight bun. Her pale skin looked out of place in the Texas heat.

"That's where we're headed next," Ellen said. "Why?"

"It's hard for me to see beyond the shadow man," she said. "Watch out for him—a shade in Santa Fe. You might want to change your travel plans."

Tanya's face became as pale as the psychic's. "Maybe we should."

"We aren't changing our plans," Ellen said. "Come on, Tanya. Pay the lady, and let's get our seats before the show."

The musical *Texas* had a full crowd on stadium-style benches made of cement. Although sitting on the bench for two hours was hard on Ellen's back, the time flew by. Most of it was spent laughing along with the crowd.

"That was a hoot," Sue said when it was over.

"Yes, but I could use a massage," Tanya said, rubbing her back.

"I have a spa day scheduled for us on Saturday in Santa Fe," Ellen said. "My treat."

"Are we sure we still want to go there?" Tanya asked. "What do you think of what the psychic said? Are we going to run into the shade of Santa Fe?"

"You still have your *gris gris* bag, don't you?" Ellen pulled hers out from beneath her blouse. It hung around her neck from a thin leather band.

"Of course," Tanya said, pulling hers out, too.

They turned to Sue.

"I'm not wearing mine. It bothers me."

"But you brought it with you, didn't you?" Ellen asked, suddenly worried.

"Yes. I sleep with it," Sue said.

"Maybe you should wear it in Santa Fe, just in case," Tanya said.

The next morning, Ellen made coffee, and she and her friends sat on the patio and watched the sunrise over the canyon. The canyon stretched as far and wide as the eyes could see and was at least 800 feet in the deepest areas. Striations of varying shades of orange, red, pink, gold, and purple created a beautiful color pallet that sparkled beneath the rising sun.

"I wish my mother could have seen this before she died," Sue said. "She loved beautiful sunrises."

"It's a shame she never made it out here," Ellen said. "The last time I was here, I painted it."

"Oh, this is the painting in your den over the sofa?" Tanya asked.

Ellen nodded. "Whenever I look at it, it brings me back here, to when the kids were little, and Paul was still alive."

"How does Brian feel about the painting?" Sue asked.

"He thinks it's beautiful—at least, that's what he says."

Ellen hoped Sue wouldn't press for more. Ellen hadn't told Brian what the painting meant to her, because she didn't want to hurt his feelings.

"Ready for our hike?" Tanya asked.

"Do pigs fly?" Sue said with a laugh.

"The sooner we do our hike, the sooner we can get on the road to Santa Fe," Ellen pointed out. "Just think, in five hours, we could be shopping in the plaza."

"Is that supposed to motivate me? That's just what I'm looking forward to, more walking."

"Oh, come on, Sue," Tanya said. "This will be more of a stroll than a hike. I promise."

Ellen and her friends put on their walking shoes and then took the trail beside their cabin into the canyon.

Ellen breathed in the cool, morning air. The beauty of the canyon elevated her mood. Some of the stone formations were thick and striated, while other rocks formed mounds of crushed granite. In the distance was a tall formation that reminded Ellen of the sphinx.

"Watch your step," Tanya said from up front as she stepped over a large rock.

"This feels so good," Ellen said from where she took up the rear. "I feel like we're one with nature."

"And nature is so majestic, isn't it?" Tanya said. "Doesn't that big rock look like the tower of a magical castle?"

"I thought it looked more like the sphinx," Ellen said.

Sue shook her head. "You see a castle and Ellen sees a sphinx. What does it say about me that I see a penis?"

Tanya scoffed. "You know what it says about you."

"Don't tell Tom," Sue warned. "He'll say my mind is in the gutter."

"Isn't it?" Ellen asked.

"Yes, but there's no need for Tom to know that."

The three friends chuckled. Ellen realized that if someone had overheard Sue, they might think she was a promiscuous woman who hid her extramarital interests from her husband, but her friends knew she just liked to make people laugh.

Tanya asked, "You think there's any truth to what that psychic said about there being a shade in Santa Fe? What if there is? What if he confronts us?"

"Oh, Tanya," Sue said, "you know as well as we do that there are ghosts everywhere. I'm sure there's more than one shade in Santa Fe."

"But why would the psychic warn us?" Tanya wanted to know.

"If anyone can handle a confrontation with a ghost, it's us," Sue said. "Don't let fear get in your way of having a good time."

Ellen heard a shriek as Tanya stopped short.

"Tanya? What are you screaming about?" Ellen asked from the rear.

"That wasn't me," Tanya said, backing up. "It was that tarantula. See it?"

On the trail two feet in front of Tanya, a hairy tarantula stood on its hind legs shrieking like a small child. The spider was as big as Ellen's hand.

"Turn back" Sue said, as she pushed Ellen in the direction from which they'd come. "I've had enough of nature for one day."

"So much for not letting fear get in the way of having a good time," Ellen teased.

"I can handle just about anything but a hairy spider," Sue said. "Especially one that screams."

CHAPTER TWO

The House on Luna Circle

Ellen and her friends checked into La Fonda, a historical hotel full of shops and restaurants, around four o'clock on Thursday and, after an early dinner, walked around the plaza. Tanya bought a turquoise ring from one of the Native Americans selling beneath the portico that stretched across the façade of the oldest public building in the U.S.—the Palace of the Governors.

At a corner shop across from the Loretto Chapel, Sue found a gorgeous purse that had been handwoven by a Native American, with plenty of room for her gun, saltshaker, and other necessities. Ellen didn't find anything she wanted for herself, but when they re-entered La Fonda from another entrance, she saw a life-size alpaca made of cotton and alpaca wool and decorated with colorful pom-poms and tassels. It was just outside one of the La Fonda giftshops. She bought it for Alison, knowing her daughter would adore it.

Later in her room, Ellen phoned Brian to check in with him. She told him about Palo Duro Canyon, the psychic, the musical, the tarantula, and the alpaca she bought. It was nice to have someone to whom she could tell the details of her trip.

She hadn't yet told him the real reason why she had come to Santa Fe.

On Friday morning, Ellen drove her friends to the vacant house on Luna Circle, where they were to meet the realtor.

"The street is very private," Sue said as Ellen pulled up to the curb. "You won't get much traffic."

"And you have amazing views of the mountains in every direction," Tanya said.

"Which is a good thing, since the front yard isn't much to look at," Ellen said of the neglected yard.

"Well, you can fix that," Tanya pointed out.

"Or hire someone else to do it," Sue said.

Mostly dirt, the lot was cut into the hillside, with a tall retaining wall on the right. The hill was so high that the neighbor's house couldn't be seen from below. The hill sloped steeply to the left, and although the house on that side was visible, it was mainly the flat adobe-style roof and driveway and not the façade.

A shorter retaining wall framed the perimeter of the front yard next to the driveway. Ellen thought it would make a beautiful planting bed, but currently it resembled a sandbox.

The house itself was a single-story, modern-looking building made of adobe but painted white with blue trim. There was a large picture window on the left and a one-car garage on the right at the end of a long driveaway. Steps led up to a small, covered porch in the center with just enough room for the porch swing, which was painted in the same color blue as the trim.

The realtor pulled up beside the rental, so Ellen and her friends hopped out.

"Ellen McManius?" the woman asked.

The woman had straight black hair that fell to her shoulders and intense black eyes. She appeared to be in her late thirties.

Ellen stepped forward. "That's me. Nancy?"

The woman nodded. "It's nice to meet you."

Ellen offered her hand for a shake. "It's nice to meet you, too. These are my friends, Tanya and Sue."

"Hello," her friends said.

"Hello." The realtor gave them a friendly nod. "Do you have any questions about the property before we take a look inside?"

"I have a question," Sue said. "How long has this house been vacant?"

"Since the last owner died in 2002," Nancy said.

"Wow, that's a long time," Tanya said. "He didn't die in the house, did he?"

"No. He was in a car accident."

"No one else died in the house, did they?" Tanya asked. "Nothing evil has happened here?"

"I've not been told so," the realtor said, as she scratched the side of her arm.

"It's in a great location." Ellen looked around at the mountains on the horizon. "Why hasn't it sold?"

"Well, this property butts up to a dog park," Nancy said. "That puts off a lot of buyers."

"Oh, that explains it," Ellen said, now having second thoughts about the house.

"I don't hear any dogs," Sue said.

"That's just it," Nancy said. "You probably wouldn't hear them. Why don't we look inside, and then I'll show you how far back the property line is?"

"Sounds good." Ellen followed Nancy up the steps.

"This is quaint," Tanya said of the porch.

"Yes, it is." Nancy unlocked the door. "The house was built in 1953, which is reflected in the mid-century architecture."

Ellen followed Nancy into a sunken living room that stretched deeper than it was wide, all the way to the back exterior of the home, where three floor-to-ceiling windows offered a pretty view of the up-sloping hill behind the house and the mountains beyond. At least the dog park wasn't visible from the house.

"The natural light from those windows would be great for painting, wouldn't it?" Tanya asked.

"It sure would," Ellen said.

"Are you an artist?" Nancy asked Ellen.

"Not a serious one," Ellen said. "It's more of a hobby."

"She's an exceptional artist," Sue said.

"Then you'd fit right in," Nancy said. "I'm sure you're aware that Santa Fe is full of talented people. In fact, while you're here, you should check out Meow Wolf, if you haven't already. It's an artist's delight."

"I bought us tickets for later today," Ellen said.

"Oh, good," Nancy said. "You're in for a treat." Then she added, "There are two bedrooms and a bath to the left. The garage, utility room, and master suite are to your right, just on the other side of the kitchen/dining combo. I had the water turned on to show you that all the plumbing works."

Ellen stepped up from the sunken living room to a dining area with an old linoleum floor. At the front of the house was an open concept kitchen. It was small and dated but had good bones. The sink sat below a small window looking out to the front of the property. She turned on the faucet, and water sputtered out before forming a smooth stream.

"I'd rip up this carpet," Sue called from the living room. "Any chance there's a wooden floor beneath it?"

"I'm afraid not," Nancy replied.

Tanya shrugged. "Ellen can easily have wood or tile installed."

"I believe the last renovations were done in the late seventies," Nancy said.

A pair of sliding glass doors led from the dining area to the back yard, but Ellen wanted to check out the other rooms before going outside. The master bedroom was a bit small, as was the master bath. They would do for an artist's retreat. What mattered was the lighting in the main room. She checked out the garage. Just as she had hoped, there were no windows, which meant her paintings would be safe from fading if stored there.

The utility room, situated between the master suite and the garage, was surprisingly large and would provide more storage for art supplies. Ellen crossed through the sunken living room to the opposite side of the house. Both the bedroom in the front and the one in back had large windows with mountain views, and the bathroom between them, though small and in need of a complete gut, had a good layout.

"I know which room I want." Sue stepped from the back bedroom. "This one has the best views of the mountains."

"Now, hold on," Ellen said beside Sue in the small hallway between the bedrooms. "If I get this place, I'm sure I'll have you come out here with me every once in a while, but it's meant to be a getaway—and not just from Brian."

"Well, if that's how you feel, why did you invite us along?" Tanya asked from the dining area.

"Because I value your opinion," Ellen said as she stepped into the sunken living area.

"This has nothing to do with ghosts, right?" Tanya asked. "Because I thought we put that behind us."

"Right," Ellen said. She turned to Nancy. "Has anyone complained about paranormal activity in this home?"

"Not that I'm aware of," Nancy said.

Ellen lifted her palms to Tanya. "See?"

"Not that she's aware of," Tanya repeated. "That's not the same as *no*."

Ellen turned back to Nancy. "Can we take a look outside?"

"Of course." Nancy opened the sliding glass doors.

"I would replace these with French doors," Sue said as she followed Ellen out onto a flat patio.

Made of flagstone, the patio wasn't covered. Ellen was glad for that because it meant more natural light inside. It also offered another airy spot for Ellen to paint.

A bench made of concrete had been left behind, along with empty pots for planting. A stone retaining wall, like the one on the right side of the house and around the perimeter of the front yard, offered more seating. The retaining wall framed the patio—except for the opening in the center back, where a set of steps were built into the hillside.

The rocky hillside ascended at a nearly forty-five-degree slope without a fence in sight. Ellen couldn't see fences to her right or left either. With a few scattered trees, it was a beautiful natural landscape that met the mountains at the horizon and gave one the feeling that there was nobody else around. Ellen liked that. That was just what she was looking for in a retreat: the feeling of isolation surrounded by a beautiful landscape while having easy access to nearby shops and restaurants.

"What about drainage?" Sue asked as she stared up the hill. "Where does all the rain go?"

"I'll show you, if you'll follow me."

Nancy began to climb the two dozen or so steps built into the hillside. The steps were made from railroad ties.

"I might just wait for you all down here," Sue said. "I'll test out this bench."

"Thanks for your help, Sue," Ellen said with a chuckle as she ascended the hillside after Nancy.

"I'm always happy to lend a helping hand," Sue said.

As Ellen reached the summit of the hill, a ravine came into view. According to Nancy, it marked the end of the property and dropped about sixty feet to a dry riverbed.

"No drainage problems here," Nancy pointed out.

There was an old steel bridge that ran across the narrow ravine leading to the dog park on the other side. The park appeared to be acres of desert hills spotted with clusters of mesquite trees and shrubs. Now that they were on top of the hill, Ellen could hear an occasional bark, but that hadn't been the case below. She doubted the dogs would bother her.

Ellen approached the bridge and turned to Nancy. "Is this thing safe?"

"As far as I know," Nancy said.

"I wouldn't trust it," Tanya warned. "It's giving me a creepy feeling."

Ellen had the same feeling, like a Spidey sense warning her to stay off the bridge.

"Who owns the bridge?" she asked. "Whose responsibility is it to maintain?"

"If you were to buy this house, it would be your responsibility," Nancy said. "It was put there in 1955 by the original owner, so he could have easy access to the trails that eventually became the Frank S. Ortiz Dog Park."

Ellen nodded. "Good. That's the first thing I'll do—have an engineer look at it."

"Does that mean you want to make an offer?" Nancy asked.

Ellen grinned. "Yes, I think so."

After lunch, Ellen and her friends returned to their respective rooms at the La Fonda for a rest. They planned to meet up in an hour before heading to Meow Wolf. Ellen took the opportunity to call Brian to tell him about her plans to put an offer on the house on Luna Circle.

"I don't understand," Brian said. "Are you trying to tell me something?"

"I just thought it would be nice to have an artist's retreat in the city of artists."

"If you're having second thoughts about us, I can move back to the house in Portland. You don't have to buy a house in Santa Fe."

Ellen sighed. "I'm not having second thoughts, Brian. I promise. I'm just used to having more of my own space."

There was silence on the other end.

"I'd love for you to fly out and see it before I make the offer," she added.

"I don't think that's necessary," he said. "It's your retreat, not mine."

"Please don't be angry with me," Ellen said.

"I'm not angry. Just unnerved. I've never been in a relationship where I wasn't the one needing more space."

"It's an adjustment for both of us," she said. "We'll find our mojo."

"I hope so, Ellen."

When Ellen ended the call, she felt a knot forming in her stomach. They would find their mojo, wouldn't they?

CHAPTER THREE

Meow Wolf

When Ellen and her friends arrived at Meow Wolf, there was a line waiting to get inside, even though everyone had prepaid tickets. They waited for nearly fifteen minutes on a sidewalk beneath a canopy in the dry heat with a dozen other tourists. Once they entered, there was a sign that read *The House of Eternal Return*. Ellen and her friends handed over their tickets at a counter before entering a dark corridor.

The corridor opened to the façade of a two-story house with a covered porch.

"Well, this is different," Sue said.

Tanya led the way. "Let's check it out."

Ellen followed Tanya onto the porch and through the front door into what at first looked like a typical two-story home. They were about to climb the staircase when a father and daughter popped out from a Harry-Potter-like cupboard beneath it.

"Is that a closet?" Sue asked.

"You'll see," the father said. "I don't want to spoil it."

"Let's start upstairs," Ellen, who had already begun ascending the steps behind Tanya, called to Sue.

"Alright," Sue said. "But these stairs don't seem very solid."

"Hundreds, if not thousands, of people have visited this place, and they've held up this long," Ellen said.

Sue chuckled. "Is that supposed to reassure me? Because it sounds like they may need a pick-me-up."

When they reached the top, Tanya led them through a series of bedrooms, which, at first glance, appeared to be average-looking, but, upon closer inspection, contained whimsical and strange elements. One had a bookcase with a secret entrance. Another held a diary full of details about time travel. In another, Ellen looked inside a closet and found a passageway to a wintery cave with colorful creatures hanging above her. Although Tanya and Sue had already moved on, Ellen decided to take a closer peek inside the cave.

She wandered down a ramp to the bottom floor where the faces of interesting creatures looked back at her. She was about to turn to look for her friends when she saw a globe-shaped spacecraft sitting in a nook in front of a mirror filled with lights. As she gazed at the interesting feature, with all its buttons and gadgets inside, she smiled at the reflection of a young Asian man standing behind her. His eyes were red, as if they'd been irritated by allergies or smoke.

"Isn't this interesting?" she said, turning toward him, but there was no one behind her.

Bewildered, she glanced left and right. To her right, she saw the back of someone that might have been him. Out of curiosity, she decided to follow him.

He led her into what appeared to be a room at the bottom of the sea. It was filled with colorful coral. Fish hung from the ceiling. And mirrors made the space appear infinite on both sides. A statue of a diver in an old 1950's diver suit—looking more like an astronaut than a diver— stood in the tall, colorful coral, and two teens were having their photo taken with it. Ellen caught her reflection in the mirror behind the coral, and there, standing behind her again, was the Asian man.

Ellen gasped and turned to face him. Again, he was gone.

Could this be the shade of Santa Fe that the psychic had warned her and her friends about?

Ellen turned and saw his back as he left the sea room. She followed.

He led her through a narrow corridor, where a bookcase opened to reveal another secret room. It was made of bottlecaps. Ellen didn't spend any time studying the interesting patterns of the room, because the man—or shade—had slipped into another corridor, where colorful lines shot out from a focal point, creating an optical illusion. She followed the man through a room made of candy and then up a metal ladder to a treehouse.

"Wait!" she cried, just before he turned into another room—a kitchen that was painted in black and white stripes. Even the dishware, the sink, and the stove were striped.

She hurried across the treetops to another room, where she lost sight of the man. The facades of small-town buildings lined the left and right of the space. Not knowing which way to go, she hesitated before descending a metal ladder into a dark room where a harp made of red laser beams was being strummed by a family. Ellen hurried through the room in search of the shade of Santa Fe.

She shrieked when she reached an enormous Yeti glaring down at her. Luckily, no one had been around to witness her making a fool of herself. From there, she entered a room where a kid used a mallet to hit the brightly colored ribs of a dinosaur to produce musical notes. Across the room, Ellen saw the back of the man. She followed him.

"Wait!" she cried again.

She entered a dark tunnel and emerged in a room that paid tribute to disco and had vibrant seventies colors—like orange, lime green, and yellow, along with a woman dancing on a television screen. From there, Ellen entered an RV as she caught sight of the man leaving the vehicle on the other side. She followed him to find herself in what appeared to be a dead end.

Where had the man—or shade—gone?

Then she noticed that a wooden panel at the very back of the room was cut in the same shape as the door leading to the cupboard beneath the stairs. She pushed on it to find herself back to where she had started, just inside the House of Eternal Return.

Geez, it was like a nightmare.

Having lost sight of the man, Ellen wandered through a strange dining room on the first floor of the house and into a kitchen, where a little girl had opened the refrigerator to reveal yet another secret entrance to more bizarre places. Ellen was enthralled by a refrigerator acting as a portal to more rooms. Beyond the girl holding the door to the refrigerator was the Asian man peering at Ellen in the reflection of a wall of mirrors. He laughed silently at her before he dashed out of view.

Ellen pushed her way into the refrigerator and cried, "Who are you?"

Sue emerged from around the bend of the brightly lit mirrored room. "Ellen? Who are you talking to?"

"Follow that man. Did you see him?"

Sue furrowed her brows. "No. I'm the only one back here. I've been lost for nearly an hour. I can't find my way out of this maze. Will you help me?"

"You didn't see an Asian man hurry past you just now?" Ellen asked again as she entered the round white room full of mirrors.

"No. It's just me. Shouldn't we be going toward the refrigerator door and not away from it? And isn't this the craziest thing you've ever seen?"

Ellen looked at herself in one of the mirrors. The reflection of the Asian man stared back at her from behind her shoulder. Her mouth fell open and her heart drummed against her ribs as she stared back at him. Quickly, she turned. There was no one there.

"Let's get out of here," Ellen said to Sue.

"Lead the way."

That evening, Ellen and her friends ate at Tortilla Flats, where they ordered cheese enchiladas with black beans and sopapillas. Ellen had decided not to say anything about the shade. Tanya would undoubtedly worry about the psychic's warning.

After their food arrived, Ellen took one bite of her enchilada and then quickly drank down her iced tea.

"Too spicy!" she said to her friends. "There's no way I can eat this."

"It's definitely not Tex-Mex," Tanya agreed. "Now I wish I would have ordered the tortilla soup."

"Well, these sopapillas are the size of a dinner plate," Sue said. "I bet one of these will hold you over while you order a bowl."

Ellen and Tanya did that very thing and then watched in awe as Sue managed to eat the spicy enchiladas.

"I hope you don't get heartburn tonight," Ellen said.

"I've already thought of that and took a preemptive Pepcid," Sue said.

By the time Ellen had finished her sopapilla, she was no longer hungry for the bowl of soup. When the waitress brought it out, she asked if she could get it to go. Tanya did the same.

"How would y'all feel about driving by the house on Luna Circle tonight before we return to La Fonda?" Ellen asked. "I'd like to see if people are still out with their dogs and if they can be heard near the house."

"Sure," Sue said. "I saw a bakery on the way where we could get a slice of pie and a cup of coffee afterward."

"Sounds like a plan," Tanya said.

CHAPTER FOUR

A Cry for Help

Ellen parked the rental in front of the adobe house on Luna Circle. Using the flashlights on their phones, she and her friends walked around to the back of the house.

"It sounds pretty quiet out here," Sue said.

"I can't even hear traffic," Tanya said. "That's a plus."

"I think I'll climb up the hill and see if there are still people at the park," Ellen said. "It's a Friday night. I want to make sure that it isn't used by teens for drinking and partying and whatnot."

"Good idea," Tanya said. "I'll go with you."

"I'll test out this concrete bench again," Sue said.

Ellen chuckled as she led Tanya up the steps to the top of the hill.

"I smell lavender," Ellen said.

"That's me, remember? I told you I've been using this new lavender skin cream."

"That's right. It smells nice."

"You should try it. I'm really into lavender right now. It helps with so many problems. The cream helps with my eczema. The aromatherapy helps with pain, hot flashes, and respiratory health. And the tea, which I've been drinking almost every night, helps with anxiety. I really wish you and Sue would try it. I know I've mentioned it to you before."

"You have. I remember now. I promise to give it a try."

When they reached the top, Tanya gazed out across the ravine. "I don't see anyone out there. Do you?"

"No," Ellen said, relieved. "And it's quiet up here, which is nice."

"Look at all those stars." Tanya turned her face up to the sky. "It's dark enough out here to see them. That's unusual this close to a city center."

Ellen gazed up to see hundreds of bright dots illuminating the night sky. "True." And down below, in the direction of the house, she could see the lights of the plaza.

Just then, Ellen heard something. It sounded like a person crying.

"Do you hear that?" Tanya asked her.

Ellen glanced around with her flashlight. "Where's it coming from?"

"Help! Help me!" someone cried.

"It's coming from the ravine!" Tanya rushed to the bridge and shined her light down into the narrow gorge along the dry riverbed.

Ellen did the same and shouted, "Hello?"

"Help me!"

"It sounds like a woman," Tanya said.

"Where are you?" Ellen cried. "I don't see you!"

"I'm trapped! Please help!"

"I'm calling 9-1-1," Ellen said as she tapped on her phone.

"9-1-1, is this an emergency?" the dispatcher asked.

"Yes. My name is Ellen McManius. I'm at the ravine behind 1124 Luna Circle. I hear a woman crying out for help. I think she's trapped somewhere below the bridge."

"Hold one moment, please," the dispatcher said.

"Any sign of her?" Ellen asked Tanya, who continued shining her light along the ravine.

"Not yet."

"Help is on the way," the dispatcher said. "Can you stay on the phone with me until the first responders arrive?"

"Yes." To Tanya, she said, "You better let Sue know what's going on. Can you meet the firetruck and send them up here?"

"Sure. What are you going to do?" Tanya asked.

"I'll keep looking for the woman from up here. I'll stay on the phone with 9-1-1 until help arrives."

Tanya descended the hill as Ellen put the phone on speaker so she could shine the light into the ravine below the old bridge.

"Are you still on the phone?" the dispatcher asked.

"Yes, I'm here."

"When was the last time you heard the cry for help?"

"Just a minute ago."

"Why don't you try to make contact with her again?"

"Okay," Ellen said. Then, into the ravine, she cried, "Are you still there?"

"Ask for her name," the dispatcher said. "And let her know that help is coming."

"Can you hear me?" Ellen cried again.

"Help me!"

"Help is on the way," Ellen said. "Can you tell me your name?"

"Angie. Please help. I'm trapped down here."

"Angie what? What's your last name?"

"Angie Cole."

Into the phone, Ellen said, "Did you hear that? Her name is Angie Cole."

"Ask her how long she's been there," the dispatcher said.

Suddenly, Ellen's phone died.

In the distance, Ellen heard sirens. It sounded like a firetruck headed her way.

Into the ravine, Ellen shouted, "Angie? How long have you been trapped down there?"

There was no reply.

"Help is coming," Ellen said again. "Angie? Can you hear me?"

Again, there was no answer.

Ellen turned to see Tanya running up the steps followed by three firefighters and two paramedics.

"This way!" Ellen cried to the first responders. "Her name is Angie Cole and she's trapped down there."

One of the paramedics said, "Why don't you wait for us at the house, and we'll update you as soon as we can?"

"Okay. Thanks."

Ellen followed Tanya back to the patio where Sue was waiting.

"Did they find her?" Sue asked.

"They're just getting started," Tanya said.

Ellen paced for half an hour before the paramedics descended the hill and one of them said, "We still haven't found her."

"How can she be that hard to find?" Sue wondered. "The ravine isn't that deep."

"Well, it's sixty feet, according to the realtor," Tanya pointed out.

"But still," Sue insisted. "There are only so many places she could be."

"They're still looking," the other paramedic said. "Why don't you ladies go home, and we'll call you with an update as soon as possible."

Sue gave the paramedic her number, since Ellen's phone was dead. Then the ladies returned to their hotel after picking up slices of pie. In the lobby of La Fonda, they ate tortilla soup and pie as they waited to hear back from the paramedics.

"It doesn't make any sense," Tanya said before slurping her soup from a plastic spoon. "She sounded like she was right below the bridge. Why haven't they found her by now?"

"I'm wondering the same thing," Ellen said.

Sue took out her phone. "What did you say the woman's name was?"

"Angie Cole," Ellen said.

Ellen watched Sue tap on her phone.

"Well, this is strange," Sue said.

"What is?" Tanya asked.

"According to this obituary, Angela Cole of Santa Fe died at age thirty-five ten years ago."

Ellen's mouth fell open. "It couldn't have been the same Angie, could it have been?"

"That would explain why the first responders can't find her," Tanya said.

"And why my phone died," Ellen murmured.

Just then, Sue's phone rang.

"Hello?" Sue asked, putting the phone on speaker.

"Mrs. McManius?" a man on the other end asked.

"Yes?" Ellen said.

"This is fire chief Greg Grayson calling to let you know that we conducted a thorough search of the ravine tonight and found no traces of a trapped victim. We'll look again in the morning, but I suspect it may have been the wind. It makes strange noises through these gorges, and it wouldn't be the first time someone mistook it for the sound of a human voice."

"But we heard more than just a cry," Ellen said. "She told me her name, Angie Cole."

"We'll look again in the morning and update you then. Good night."

Ellen and her friends looked at one another with bewilderment. Had a ghost reached out to them tonight?

"What if Angie needs our help?" Sue said. "If she's trapped, maybe something is keeping her from moving on."

"I thought those days were behind us," Tanya said. "But I guess I can't turn my back on a soul in need of peace."

Ellen smiled and shook her head. "I really didn't bring you here for this. I promise."

"We know," Sue said. "But as long as we're here, don't you think it's our duty to help, if we can?"

"You don't think it's a shadow man messing with us, do you?" Tanya wondered.

"No," Ellen said, though she'd wondered the same thing.

"Let's find out what we can about Angie Cole in the morning and go from there," Sue said.

"Okay," Tanya said.

"Sounds good."

That night as Ellen readied for bed in her hotel bathroom, brushing her teeth and then removing her eye makeup, the Asian man appeared in the mirror behind her.

She froze for several seconds, unable to speak, unable to breathe. Her hands began to shake, and she felt her knees about to give out beneath her.

When she could, she said, "Who are you, and what do you want?"

He lifted his chin and laughed silently in the mirror.

Slowly, she turned, but as before, no one was there.

Quickly, she put on a robe and grabbed her purse, phone, and key card and darted down the hall without shoes to Sue's room, where she knocked on the door.

"What's up?" Sue asked. "Has something happened?"

"Can I come in?" Ellen asked.

"Of course," Sue stepped inside so Ellen could follow her into the room.

"Grab that chair from the window," Sue said.

"You have a better view than I do," Ellen said, trying to calm her nerves. She grabbed one of two club chairs from an alcove with a large window overlooking the plaza.

Sue sat in an armchair upholstered in a southwestern print with a matching ottoman. She put up her feet and said, "Yes, I guess I'm the lucky one this time. So, tell me what's got you all frazzled. Did you and Brian have an argument?"

Ellen moved the club chair so that she was facing Sue when she sat in it. "No. It's nothing like that."

"Are your kids alright?"

"Yes. Yes, they're fine. Remember when we were at Meow Wolf inside the refrigerator, and I asked you if you'd seen a man?"

"Yes. I thought that was kind of strange. Had he offended you in some way?"

"No. I kept seeing him with my reflection in the mirrors, but when I'd turn, he'd disappear."

Sue narrowed her eyes. "Why didn't you mention this before?"

"I don't know. I thought maybe I'd imagined it. And I didn't want to worry Tanya."

"Did you see him again tonight? Is that what's frazzled you?"

Ellen nodded. "In the bathroom mirror. I know it's a lot to ask, but, well, can I sleep in here with you tonight?"

"For all we know, he may have followed you here."

"I thought of that. I still carry a shaker of salt in my purse. We could make a circle of protection around the bed."

"Well. It's a good thing I got a room with a king-sized bed. This would have been awkward if we'd had to share a double."

"Thank you. I don't know why he's following me."

Sue crossed her arms. "Could this be the shade of Santa Fe? The one the psychic warned us about?"

"Maybe. I don't know. He's not like Angie. He's not asking for my help."

"How do you know?"

"He just laughs at me. It's creepy. Otherwise, I would have stayed in my room and made the circle of protection there. But this man has me spooked."

"And now I'm spooked, too. Thanks a lot."

"Sorry."

"It's okay. I know you'd do the same for me if I had a man following me around—unless he were good looking," she teased, "in which case, I would want him to follow me around. Is your shade good looking?"

"All except for his red eyes. He's a young Asian man—tall and thin with a devilish smile."

"Sounds like my type," Sue teased again.

Ellen grinned as she took the saltshaker from her purse. "I'll make the circle."

As they readied for bed, Sue said, "I did a little more research on Angie Cole. It was hard to find her cause of death, but I finally figured it out when I found her Facebook page."

"What was it?" Ellen asked.

"Suicide."

Ellen frowned. "Oh, how sad. Are you sure it was the same Angie Cole?"

"Pretty sure. Angie West Cole. Born and raised here. She left behind two little boys and a husband of six years," Sue said.

"Depression is such a horrible and misunderstood illness," Ellen said.

"That's the strange part," Sue said. "According to what people wrote on her Facebook page, her suicide was completely unexpected. There were no signs of depression."

"You'd think someone would have noticed that something was up."

"I think this happens more often than we might realize."

"I wonder if that's why she's trapped," Ellen said. "Maybe she has unfinished business."

"We should go there again tomorrow evening, after our spa day," Sue said. "But lord knows how I'm going to make it up that hill."

"We could try our séance on the back patio. Maybe we can reach her from there."

"I guess we'll find out tomorrow night."

CHAPTER FIVE

Spa Day

Morning came early for Ellen when her phone alarm went off at 8:00. She'd set it to give her time to shower and dress for breakfast, but between her fear of the shade of Santa Fe and Sue's snoring, she hadn't gotten much sleep.

Afraid to return to her room alone, she woke up Sue.

"What's wrong?" Sue mumbled without opening her eyes.

"I need you to take your shower now so you can come to my room while I take mine."

Sue buried her face in her pillow. "What are you talking about?"

"I don't want to shower in my room alone, just in case the shade of Santa Fe visits me again."

Sue sighed. "Why don't you shower here while I sleep?"

"All my stuff is in my room."

"Go get it real fast. I bet you can outrun him."

Ellen was tempted to throw her pillow at her friend, but, instead, she built up her nerve and returned to her room. She began to gather her things but then thought she was overreacting. Maybe she'd rather face the shade than lug her cosmetic case and clothes over to Sue's.

Quickly, she stripped and jumped into the shower. She kept her eyes open, even when she rinsed her face. She didn't want to open them just to be shocked by his arrival. She wanted to see him coming.

Within fifteen minutes she was dressed and ready, with makeup on and hair fixed. Not wanting to push her luck, she decided to wait for her friends at the restaurant rather than spend another moment alone. She made a mental note to find an incense shop where she might buy a sage smudge stick to cleanse her room. Once she was downstairs and seated, she texted Sue and Tanya to let them know where she was.

While she waited for her friends, she looked for Angie West Cole's Facebook page on her phone, hoping to learn more about the restless spirit that was trapped in the ravine behind the house on Luna Circle.

The comments from grieving friends and family brought tears to her eyes. She went further back and read posts from ten years ago, leading up to Angie's death, and found nothing but joyful posts from a stay-at-home mother of two toddler boys. She and her husband appeared happy. People didn't always post about their demons on Facebook. You couldn't judge a person's true disposition from their page. However, it was nevertheless baffling to see no sign of distress among the perfectly happy posts by the then young mother and wife.

Ellen's research was interrupted by a phone call from Nancy Aguilar, her real estate agent, letting her know that the offer had been accepted.

"Congratulations," Nancy said. "Barring no major surprises during the inspection, the house is yours."

"Wonderful," Ellen said. "Thanks. When is the inspection?"

"I'll have the electricity turned on and schedule someone to go out there in two days."

"Great. Thanks."

As Ellen ended the call, Sue and Tanya appeared and sat at the table with her.

"I thought you were coming back," Sue said as she picked up a menu. "Or did I dream that conversation we had this morning?"

"What conversation?" Tanya asked.

For the second time that morning, Ellen had the desire to throw something at Sue. "Um—"

"Ellen borrowed my curling iron," Sue said quickly, after realizing her mistake. "I thought she was going to bring it back."

"Since when do you use a curling iron?" Tanya asked Ellen.

"Um, I guess this dry heat made my hair, I don't know, flat."

"Why are you two lying to me?" Tanya demanded.

The waitress arrived to take their order, and Ellen thought she was off the hook, but Tanya said, "Could you please give us a few more minutes?"

"Of course," the waitress said.

Alone again, Tanya said, "Spill."

"Don't be upset with me," Ellen began, "but there's something I need to tell you."

Ellen told Tanya about the shade of Santa Fe—how he appeared to her at Meow Wolf and then again last night in her hotel room. She admitted to having spent the night with Sue with a circle of protection around the bed.

Tanya's face turned pale, and she frowned and turned her attention to the menu. But Ellen could tell Tanya wasn't reading it.

"I just didn't want to worry you," Ellen said. "I'm sorry I didn't say anything before."

"You know how I hate it when you do that," Tanya said. "You keep me out of the loop because you think I can't handle it. You think I'm weak, but I'm not. There's a difference between being frightened and being weak."

"We know," Sue said. "We don't think you're weak."

"I just want us to be careful, that's all," Tanya said. "I've helped ghosts just as much as you have."

"You're right," Ellen said. "I'm so sorry I didn't say anything sooner."

"The only reason she told me was because she was terrified to sleep alone," Sue said.

"That's right," Ellen said.

"Next time, go to Tanya's room when a ghost is haunting you," Sue said to Ellen.

Tanya's face turned a shade paler. "Okay, I admit that I understand why you chose to go to Sue's. I guess I should thank you for that, Ellen."

"Well, after that attachment," Ellen began, "I—"

"I get it. I'm not mad. Really. Let's order breakfast and put it behind us."

After they gave the waitress their order—Sue got Belgian waffles, Ellen an omelet, and Tanya oatmeal and fruit—the fire chief called Sue to let them know that after another hour of searching that morning, no victim was found. Sue relayed this information to Ellen and Tanya.

"It had to be a ghost," Tanya said. "I know it wasn't the wind."

"Tonight, at dusk, we'll see if Angie will talk to us again," Ellen said.

Since the spa was only a block away from La Fonda, Ellen and her friends did a little more shopping after breakfast. Ellen bought Santa Fe t-shirts for Nolan, Taylor, Lane, and Brian and a pair of turquoise earrings for herself. Across from the Loretto Chapel, she found a shop that sold handmade maracas, pipes, and, among other things, sage smudge sticks, so she bought a pack of three and a book of matches. Then she and her friends made their way to the spa for their eleven o'clock appointment.

The spa was brightly lit with a section for facials and skin care on the left and pedicures and manicures on the right. Two women were already being helped at the facial stations. One of the massage chairs lined up on the right held a woman getting her feet scrubbed. A silent television on the wall above the facial stations played HGTV with the captions.

Ellen had tried to talk her friends into getting full body massages, but neither Sue nor Tanya liked for people to touch their bodies. Sue preferred getting pedicures, especially since her feet always hurt. This spa had a Treat-Your-Feet service that included a thirty-minute foot massage along with the pedicure, to total one hour of luxurious treatment.

Tanya didn't like pedicures, though, because she didn't trust the technicians when it came to spreading funguses and bacteria. So, Tanya wanted a facial and a hand massage.

When her name was called, Ellen followed her massage therapist, Kelly, to one of the private rooms in back. Kelly didn't look much younger than Ellen, but she was in amazingly great shape, and her skin glowed. She wore her brown hair braided, and bangs swept across her pretty, brown eyes. Her summer dress tied around her neck and was backless, exposing three interesting tattoos. One of them read, "STAY HUMANE."

The room smelled of lavender and was dimly lit with candles. Soothing music played overhead. The massage table was covered with fresh linens.

"You can hang your clothes on the hook behind this door," Kelly said. "I'll be back in just a moment."

Ellen undressed and hung up her clothes. Then she climbed onto the table on her stomach and covered herself with the top sheet. She put her face in the donut pillow and closed her eyes. She had dozed off when Kelly knocked on the door.

"Come in," Ellen said, drowsily.

As Kelly started on Ellen's back, Ellen sighed and sunk more deeply onto the table, relaxing the muscles she didn't know she'd been clenching. Not wanting to fall asleep and miss the massage altogether, Ellen decided to start up a conversation.

"I just put an offer on a house here in Santa Fe."

"Congratulations," Kelly said. "You'll love it here. I've lived here for over thirty years, and I wouldn't move for anything."

"Well, I'm not actually moving here," Ellen explained. "I'm buying it for a studio retreat. I'm an artist. I paint."

"How nice," Kelly said. "What kind of art do you make?"

"Mostly portraits and landscapes. Whatever inspires me. I'm not a serious painter. It's more of a hobby."

"And in what area are you buying?"

"It's on Luna Circle, right behind the Frank S. Ortiz Dog Park," Ellen said. "In the Casa Solano Subdivision."

"I know the area well. I take my dogs to that park every weekend. Is it the house by Suicide Bridge?"

Ellen stiffened. "What's Suicide Bridge?"

Kelly moved her hands down Ellen's back. "I didn't mean to make you anxious. Try to relax. I'm sorry I mentioned it. I just thought that the real estate agent would have had to disclose the information."

"What information?" Ellen asked.

"There's a bridge between the dog park and a house on Luna Circle that's been for sale for ages."

"Is it an old steel bridge across a narrow ravine?"

"Yes."

Kelly worked her way up Ellen's back, but it was hard for Ellen to enjoy it, because now she was anxious about the bridge.

Kelly massaged beneath Ellen's right shoulder blade and said, "Over the years, it's become known as Suicide Bridge, because, for whatever reason, that's where a lot of people have gone to take their lives."

"What do you mean by *a lot*?"

"It seems like someone does it every year for as long as I've lived here. I would guess over fifty people have died there."

"How sad. I wonder what it is about jumping from *that* bridge. Why *there*?"

"They don't jump. They hang themselves."

Ellen sucked in her lips.

Kelly moved to the left shoulder blade. "I think they do it because the media always makes such a big deal out of it. It gives these poor people a feeling of notoriety—like they won't be forgotten because they'll always be associated with the bridge."

"Did you ever know a woman named Angie Cole?" Ellen asked.

"I didn't know her personally, but I knew of her. She committed suicide at the bridge. How did you know?"

Ellen wasn't sure if she should divulge the truth. Not everyone was open to the existence of ghosts or to the ability to communicate with them. Even Ellen hadn't been for most of her life.

But then Kelly asked, "Did you sense her spirit near the house?"

"She talked to me," Ellen said. "My friend Tanya heard her too. Angie asked for our help."

"Oh, no. Poor thing hasn't moved on. I always wondered about people who commit suicide."

"I think most of them do move on," Ellen said, "but maybe Angie has unfinished business. I'm actually a paranormal investigator and have helped tethered spirits to find peace."

Ellen had been about to add that she was a *retired* paranormal investigator, but, for whatever reason, she didn't.

"So, are you going to help her?" Kelly asked.

"I'm going to try."

"Angie's widower remarried a friend of mine," Kelly said. "Do you mind if I tell her about what you said?"

"You don't think it will upset her?"

"I don't think so, especially when I tell her of your plans to help."

Kelly began working on Ellen's neck.

"That's where I carry all my stress," Ellen said. "Oh my God. That hurts and feels good at the same time. I think I'm going to cry."

Kelly worked on Ellen's neck in silence for several minutes. Ellen closed her eyes and tried to relax. The trapezoids were the tightest muscles on Ellen's body. After she'd loosened Ellen's neck muscles, Kelly continued to massage in silence on Ellen's arms and legs, and then had her flip over so she could massage the fronts of her arms, legs, head, and belly.

When the hour was up, Ellen had tears in her eyes. She hadn't realized how badly her body had been aching. She would have to be better about having massage therapy regularly.

Before she left the room so that Ellen could dress, Kelly said, "Would you be interested in talking with Angie's widower, Darren? He might be able to shed some light on why Angie can't move on."

"Absolutely," Ellen said with a smile. "That would be awesome. Do you think he'd have time to talk to me today?"

"He spends Saturdays with his wife in her gallery on Canyon Road. I'll text you the address and let him know you're stopping by."

"Thanks so much."

CHAPTER SIX

Angie Cole

While they waited in the spa for Sue's toenails to dry, Ellen told Tanya what she'd learned about Suicide Bridge.

"That's so sad and awful. Are you sure you still want to buy the property?"

Ellen shrugged. "Except for that, it's perfect in every way."

"You should ask the realtor why she didn't disclose that."

"Good idea. I'll call her now."

Ellen called Nancy and put the question to her.

There was a long pause on the other end of the phone.

"Nancy?"

"I didn't think it was relevant, because, technically, those suicides did not happen on that property," Nancy said.

"But you said the bridge was part of the property."

"No, I said it was put there by the original owner, and therefore you would be responsible for its maintenance."

"I don't understand why no one thought to take down the bridge," Ellen said, feeling frustrated.

"Before the owner put it there, people were falling to their deaths— or, now we suspect, *jumping.*"

Ellen gasped. "In that very spot?"

"Yes."

"But why?"

"There are a lot of theories about this but, unfortunately, no facts. Do you want to rescind your offer?"

Ellen sighed. "No. Let's move forward."

After lunching on chicken pesto paninis at Sam's Corner Café, Ellen and her friends took the rental to Canyon Road, which wasn't far from the plaza. Angela's Gallery was filled with paintings of the southwestern landscape and its inhabitants: flowering cacti, lizards, frogs, mountaintops, and desert valleys.

Standing together behind a high counter were a man and woman in their forties.

"By any chance, are you Darren?" Ellen asked the man.

"That's me," he said. "And this is my wife, Monica."

Ellen introduced her friends. After the introductions, Ellen said, "Kelly worked on my back today, and she mentioned you might be willing to talk about Angie."

"Yeah, no problem, but why don't we step outside?"

He led Ellen and her friends from the art gallery to a corner café, where they sat together at a table in the shade of an oak tree.

"This is where I come for my breaks," Darren said. "Do you mind if I smoke?"

"No, go ahead," Ellen said.

"They make the best lemonade here," he added. "Would you like to have some with me?"

"We just had lunch," Sue said. "But thank you. Tanya? Ellen? What about you? Are you getting anything?"

"Nothing for me," Ellen said.

"I'd like a lemonade," Tanya said.

"Okay, then I'll have one, too," Sue said. "Would either of you want to split a cupcake with me?"

"I will," Tanya said.

The waitress took their order, and, once she'd gone, Ellen said, "Darren, did Kelly tell you that we think Angie's ghost reached out to us last night?"

Darren nodded as he exhaled smoke from the cigarette.

"Can you tell us anything about the events surrounding her death?" Sue asked.

"I never believed it was suicide," he said.

Ellen glanced at her friends and then turned back to Darren. "Do you think she was murdered?"

"It had to be. She'd been out walking our dog, Rascal. Someone hung her from the bridge by the dog leash. She'd never do that to herself. And she'd never leave Rascal to fend for himself."

"Did she have any enemies?" Tanya asked.

"No. Everyone loved her. She was a kind and joyful person. Not a depressed bone in her body. She was an artist, like Monica. They became friends at the art institute and dreamed of opening a gallery together here on Canyon Road."

"Whose idea was it to name it after Angie?" Sue asked.

"Monica and I came up with that together," he said. "I know what you might be thinking, but Monica and I didn't start dating until a year or so after Angie's death. Her death is what brought us close."

"We weren't thinking anything like that," Ellen said.

"Well, I was," Sue admitted. "Thanks for clarifying."

"You aren't the only one," Darren said. "Once our relationship became public, people started suspecting me of murder. Monica, too."

Ellen studied Darren's face. Might he have killed his wife to be with Monica? Or was it possible that Monica, without Darren's knowledge, had killed Angie because she was in love with Darren?

"It wasn't suicide, but Monica and I had nothing to do with it," he said.

The waitress appeared with their order. The lemonade and cupcake looked delicious, and Ellen regretted not ordering some, but she said nothing about it, because she wanted to focus on Angie Cole.

"Did the coroner perform an autopsy?" Ellen asked.

"Yes, but there were no signs of foul play, if that's what you're getting at. She hadn't been violated. There were no signs that she struggled—or at least nothing under her fingernails."

"Has Angie ever come to you in your dreams or at your home?" Ellen asked.

"I've had plenty of dreams of Angie over the years, but they were always about the past, when she was alive, and the boys were little."

"Is there a recurring event or image that you can recall from those dreams?" Ellen asked.

Darren took a long draw from his cigarette and seemed to be deep in thought. Ellen waited in silence while Sue and Tanya ate their cupcake and sipped their lemonade.

"I can't really think of anything. The boys have dreams about her. I could ask them."

"If you don't think it would upset them," Tanya said.

"They're teenagers now. They can handle it."

"We're conducting a séance tonight near the bridge," Ellen said, studying Darren's face for his reaction. "We'll let you know if we learn anything."

"I'd be grateful," he said.

He didn't look like a man who was worried about being caught out. Then again, his easy expression could be explained by skepticism toward the supernatural and not his innocence.

Just before dusk, Ellen drove the rental to the house on Luna Circle. She and her friends were still recovering from the excitement they'd caused at La Fonda when they'd used the sage smudge sticks to cleanse their rooms of bad spirits. A horrendous sound had blared overhead.

They should have known they'd set off the fire alarm. While the rest of the guests had flooded the halls and the stairwells, making their way to the exits, Ellen and her friends had quickly finished the job. Then they'd fled the scene to visit the local Walmart.

At Walmart, they'd picked up supplies, including flashlights, extra batteries, candles, more matches, salt, an EMF detector, a Ouija Board, bottled water, a box of crackers, a bowl, a spoon, and the ingredients for Sue's famous dip. They had also splurged on a full-spectrum camera with a tripod, an electromagnetic pump, and three lawn chairs.

Sue had wanted to make peach margaritas for the occasion, but Ellen had argued that ghosts, deep ravines, and alcohol didn't make the best combination, and Tanya had agreed.

Now, Ellen parked in the driveway of the house on Luna Circle and the three friends carried their gear to the back of the house, needing to make a few trips back and forth. The patio was dark. Ellen wished she'd thought to buy a lantern to help with set up. They managed with the flashlights, though. Ellen positioned the full-spectrum camera near the sliding glass doors, pointing the camera away from the house. She widened the focus to include the patio and as much of the hill as possible.

Tanya set up the electromagnetic pump, connecting it to the battery pack, since they didn't have access to electricity. Ellen hoped to convince Angie to draw energy from the pump instead of their electronic devices.

Sue used the EMF detector and built-in thermostat to take some initial readings.

Then Tanya positioned the lawn chairs in the center of the patio while Ellen created a circle of protection with the salt. Tanya helped her to light the candles at the four cardinal points. They found the cardinal points by using a compass app on Tanya's phone. They snacked on crackers and dip as they got everything ready.

With their bottled water and food at their feet, Ellen and her friends sat close enough to hold hands, knees touching. They had the Ouija Board within reach to use if Angie was unable to speak directly to them.

"Just like old times," Sue said as she took each of their hands. "Ready?"

"Ready," Tanya said.

"I'll start." Ellen drew in a deep breath and said in a loud voice, "Spirits of the other realm, we come in peace. We mean you no harm. We've come here tonight to help. We call on the spirit of Angie Cole. Angie, if you can hear me, please draw upon the energy from our electromagnetic pump. It's the big black box sitting on the retaining wall near us. Draw energy from the pump to speak with us. You spoke to us last night and said you were trapped. We've returned to help you. Angie, are you here with us?"

Ellen felt a chill in the air as the candle on the northern point went out.

Spirits always seemed to do that—draw from flames instead of electricity. Then again, it may have been the wind, Ellen thought.

"Angie Cole," Ellen repeated, "are you here with us? If so, please speak to us. Tell us how you died."

From far off, Ellen heard, "I don't know."

Ellen and her friends looked at one another with wide eyes.

"Angie, is that you?" Ellen asked.

"Yes. Help me!" the ghost cried.

"Ask her what's the last thing she remembers," Sue whispered.

Ellen cleared her throat and shouted, "Angie? What's the last thing you remember before you became trapped?"

"I was walking Rascal—my dog."

The candle at the eastern point flickered and went out.

"The temperature has dropped by five degrees," Sue said.

"Ask her if she remembers going to the bridge," Tanya suggested.

"Angie," Ellen called. "Do you remember walking with Rascal toward Suicide Bridge?"

"No. I remember having a strange daydream. A young man in the army was being herded onto a bus. It took him to a prison. I didn't know this man, but I could feel his pain and frustration. He had served his country, and now his country was holding him captive. That's the last thing I can remember."

"Daydream?" Tanya said.

Ellen wrinkled her nose, wondering how a daydream could lead to a person's death.

"Maybe it was a vision," Sue pointed out.

"Angie, is there anything else you can remember about the man?" Ellen asked.

The candle at the western point extinguished.

"He was Japanese."

Ellen straightened her back. Could Angie's vision have anything to do with the shade of Santa Fe?

"Do you know the man's name?" Ellen asked.

"No."

At that moment, the shade of Santa Fe appeared on the hillside, at the top of the steps leading from the patio.

Ellen blinked and then whispered to her friends, "Can you see him?"

Sue and Tanya glanced around.

"Who?" Tanya asked.

"The man at the top of the hill," Ellen whispered as she stood up and dropped her friends' hands.

"Don't break the circle," Sue warned. "Ellen, what are you doing?"

Ellen paid no heed as she stepped from the circle of protection and slowly ascended the steps toward the shade.

"Ellen, please come back," Tanya said. "You're scaring me."

"Good thing we didn't bring margaritas," Sue said.

Ellen could barely hear her friends. A load roar ripped through the air around her, encircling her in a wind tunnel that lifted her hair straight up. The man was no longer standing in front of her, but she could feel his presence, his pain, his sadness, his hatred. He wanted her to see.

She reached the top of the hill and headed toward the bridge.

"Ellen!"

Ellen blinked again as the roar diminished to silence and the winds stilled. She found herself in Tanya's arms beside Suicide Bridge.

"What happened?" Ellen asked, unable to piece together how she'd gotten there.

"You nearly stepped into the ravine!" Tanya cried, as she caught her breath. "What were you doing?"

"I don't know." Ellen struggled to snap back to reality. The feeling of the shade's pain and hatred had overwhelmed her.

"Let's go back." Tanya wrapped an arm across Ellen's shoulders. "Come on."

CHAPTER SEVEN

A Possible Possession

After Ellen's close call at Suicide Bridge, she and her friends packed up their gear—all but the lawn chairs—and returned to Sue's room at La Fonda to see if anything had been captured on the full spectrum camera. They were shocked to find that voices other than Angie's had been recorded.

"They sound like whispers and moans," Tanya said. "Can you hear what they're saying?"

"Let me try slowing it down." Ellen played back part of the recording at half speed.

"Did I hear, 'This is hell'?" Tanya said with wide eyes.

"That's what I heard," Sue said. "Along with, 'We're never getting out of here,' or something like that."

"The ravine isn't a portal to hell, is it?" Tanya asked, her face pale.

Ellen didn't think that hell was an actual place. She'd always been taught that heaven and hell were states of being. But who could really know? If there were a hell, she doubted its portal existed behind her fixer upper.

She played the recording again at half speed, trying to make out the words among the multitude of half-whispers and moans.

Ellen lifted her head. "I heard, 'She's talking to them again.' Could that refer to Angie talking to us?"

Tanya lifted her brows. "Maybe."

"Wait a minute," Sue said. "What if those are the voices of the other suicide victims? Maybe they're all trapped there for the same reason."

Tanya covered her mouth. "I hope not. That would be over fifty souls, based on what Kelly told Ellen."

Ellen gnawed on her lower lip, wondering if Sue could be onto something. "Maybe they all had something in common. I think more research is in order."

"First, let's look at the rest of the recording," Sue suggested.

As they watched their footage, Ellen gasped when she saw the Asian man.

"That's the shade!" Ellen paused the recording, but not in time to capture the shade. "You saw him, too, didn't you?"

"Yes, but only for a second," Tanya said.

"Replay it," Sue said.

Ellen replayed that part of the recording and watched with her mouth hanging open. The shade appeared on the hillside, but then, as Ellen moved toward it, it disappeared.

"What's that red orb on your head?" Sue said, pointing to the monitor. "See it?"

"Could that be the shade?" Tanya said. "Could he have possessed you?"

Ellen's knees felt week. She sat on the edge of Sue's bed.

"How do you feel?" Sue asked her.

"Scared to death. How do you think I feel?"

"But you don't feel sick, do you?" Tanya asked.

"Now that I think of it, my stomach does feel a bit queasy. But that could be my nerves."

"You're probably not possessed," Sue said. "Try not to worry about it. You were wearing your *gris gris*."

Ellen lifted the little bag that hung on a leather cord around her neck.

"But she stepped out of the circle of protection," Tanya pointed out.

"Let's not jump to any conclusions yet," Sue said. "Just to be on the safe side, I don't think you should be alone tonight, Ellen."

"Do you really think I could be possessed?" Ellen's throat was suddenly dry.

"Probably not," Sue said. "But it wouldn't hurt to be vigilant tonight."

"Then, first thing tomorrow, we'll cleanse you with sage," Tanya said. "Too bad we used it all on the rooms. But we'll buy more."

Ellen went to the bathroom to splash water on her face. As she looked at herself in the mirror, she hoped to see the shade appear, because then she'd know he hadn't entered her body. When he didn't appear, she was tempted to conjure him but thought better of it and returned to her friends.

Her fear of possession gave her a glimpse of what it must have been like for Tanya a few years ago when she'd suffered from a spirit attachment. The idea of something else invading and taking control of her body was terrifying.

"Tanya," Sue said, "why don't you go back to your room and try to get some sleep, while I take the first watch? Set an alarm to relieve me in about four or five hours."

"I'm scared to go to my room alone," Tanya said. "And I'm too wired to sleep. Let's see if we can find out anything about the other victims of Suicide Bridge."

Ellen and Tanya each took a club chair while Sue sat in the armchair with her feet on the matching ottoman. They were silent for several minutes as they conducted internet searches on their phones.

"Found something," Tanya said.

"Is it a blog by a local named Teresa Castillo?" Sue asked.

"That's the one."

"I found it, too," Ellen said as she skimmed through the home page. "Teresa made it her mission to find out as much as she could about those that took their lives on Suicide Bridge."

The three friends read silently for many minutes. Tanya got up and moved to the bed, lying on her side and yawning as she continued reading.

"I'm not finding anything that connects them," Ellen said. "Are you?"

"Well, this is interesting," Sue said. "Have you noticed how many of the victims share the same last names? There are five Wests—Angie's maiden name. Four Castillos, relatives of the blogger. Five Littles, six Nishimuras, six Jenkens, seven Guerras, four Thompsons ..."

"Teresa points that out in one of her posts," Tanya said. "She interviews a psychiatrist who talks about mental illness in families. Clinical depression is hereditary."

"That's one reason," Sue said. "There might be another."

"Like what?" Ellen asked.

"I don't know. Maybe we should interview some of the living relatives."

"That's a great idea," Ellen said. "We could start with Teresa Castillo."

Throughout the night, Ellen kept waking up to assess how she felt. Although she and her friends had created a circle of protection around them for the night, it wouldn't help if the shade were already inside the circle by having possessed Ellen. Plus, her dreams were more vivid than usual and full of strange scenes from what could only be described as a concentration camp. Guards goaded her—though she wasn't herself in the dreams. So did other prisoners. She was hated and despised by all but a few. They were men, jeering at her. She may have been a man in the dreams, too.

The fact that she'd been dreaming from the point of view of a man only further alarmed her. It could be a sign of possession.

When she wasn't dreaming or assessing how she felt, she was praying, *I rebuke you, evil spirit. I rebuke you in the name of God. Leave my body. Leave this room.*

Feeling far from rested when morning came, she was anxious to buy another smudge stick to cleanse her body. She convinced her friends to walk with her to the shop before breakfast.

Ellen and her friends were standing in front of the shop bathing themselves with the smoke from a smudge stick when a priest called out to them from across the street, in front of the Loretto Chapel. He wore a look of shock on his face. He was Asian, like the shade, though older and not as tall.

"Shinigami!" he cried as he crossed the street toward them. "Hurry! Come with me!"

He motioned for them to follow him.

"What's the matter?" Sue asked him.

"Come with me," he said. He pointed to Ellen. "She has a Shinigami on her head."

Ellen and her friends glanced at one another with astonishment.

"What's a Shinigami?" Ellen asked.

"Come now," he said. "I'll help you. Follow me."

They extinguished the smudge stick and followed the priest. Ellen was confused when he led them past Loretto Chapel. Where was he taking them? He hurried along the sidewalk, crossed the street toward La Fonda, and then continued another block to the St. Francis Cathedral. People were filling the church for Sunday morning mass, but this didn't deter the priest as he led Ellen and her friends through the narthex and to the large baptismal fountain behind the pews.

"Get in," he said to Ellen. "You need to be baptized. Quickly. Have you been baptized before?"

Ellen nodded as she handed her purse and smudge stick to Sue and stepped into the cold fountain of holy water.

The priest knelt along the rim of the fountain. "All the way under."

Ellen glanced nervously at her friends and at the people passing her as they found their seats. She pinched her nose, closed her eyes, and went under. The cold water gave her chills and made her mascara run.

"I baptize you in the name of the Father, and the Son, and the Holy Spirit," the priest said. "Do you reject Satan?"

Ellen nodded.

"Do you accept the Holy Spirit into your heart?"

"Yes," she said.

He motioned for her to go under once more. When she resurfaced, the priest was praying silently over her. Then he anointed her forehead with oil.

Ellen felt lighter and grateful. She thanked the priest.

"I want to be baptized again, too," Tanya said when he had finished. She motioned toward the fountain. "May I?"

"Yes, yes, of course. But hurry. Mass is about to begin."

"I might as well, too," Sue said as she laid their purses on the floor and followed Tanya into the fountain.

The priest snapped his fingers at an altar boy. "Bring three towels."

The altar boy scurried off and returned just as Tanya and Sue re-emerged, blinking away the holy water.

"That's cold," Tanya said.

The priest asked them the same questions. After they answered yes to each, he prayed over them.

As Ellen and her friends were drying off beside the fountain, Ellen asked again, "What's a Shinigami?"

"It's hard to explain. You should come visit me at the rectory next door when you can. I'm busy today with masses and confessions, and I have catechism all day tomorrow. Can you come Tuesday afternoon, after one o'clock?"

Ellen nodded.

"We need to be quiet now," he whispered. "The procession is coming. By the way, I'm Father Yamamoto, at your service."

"It's nice to meet you," Sue whispered back.

Ellen noticed the altar boys and priests waiting to proceed down the aisle toward the altar. The organ had already begun to play an opening hymn. She and her friends returned the towels to the priest and hurried from the cathedral.

Father Yamamoto waved to them from the steps and said, "It won't take long to dry in this heat."

CHAPTER EIGHT

A Common Denominator

After a change of clothes and a few minutes with the hair dryer, Ellen met her friends in the hall outside their rooms and accompanied them downstairs to the restaurant for breakfast.

"A Shinigami is an evil demon from Japanese mythology," Sue said after they were seated, telling Ellen what she'd already learned from her own quick search on her phone.

"I read that it's a death god," Tanya said.

The waitress came with coffee and took their order.

The hot coffee warmed Ellen from the chill she'd caught from the baptism.

"I read that, too," Sue said after the waitress had gone. "But it can also be the vengeful spirit of a deceased person who is unable to move on. According to one article, a Shinigami is believed to take possession of people and cause them to commit suicide, usually by hanging."

Ellen's jaw nearly hit the table. "Maybe that's what caused Angie to take her life—the Shinigami."

Sue nodded. "It fits with what she said about the daydream of the Japanese man being incarcerated."

"And with Darren's belief that it wasn't suicide," Ellen added.

"I think we just cracked this case wide open," Sue said.

"So, how do we stop this Shinigami from taking more lives?" Tanya wondered aloud.

"We need to find out why he's vengeful," Ellen said. "And to do that, we need to continue with our plan of interviewing the families of his victims. We need to find a common denominator. From that, we can figure out what motivates the Shinigami."

"I already emailed Teresa Castillo," Sue said. "I hope she gets back to me soon."

Tanya took a sip of her coffee. "Maybe she can help us locate family members of the other victims."

Because the baptism had left Ellen feeling rejuvenated and relieved, she had the best sleep during a late morning nap. She'd slept deeply enough to dream. It hadn't been a nightmare, but it hadn't been pleasant, either. An old Japanese woman kept asking, "Is he here? I thought he was here?" And Ellen hadn't known how to answer. "Who?" Ellen had asked. But the woman only repeated her question "Is he here?"

Just before lunch, Ellen drove her friends to the address of Teresa Castillo, who lived in an apartment less than ten minutes from the plaza.

They were seated on the balcony of the second-story apartment overlooking the swimming pool, where parents and children were playing water volleyball and sunbathing on loungers.

Teresa, a young woman in her twenties, sat with Ellen, Sue, and Tanya around her patio table pouring fresh-squeezed lemonade into glasses.

"I'm afraid it's not much," she said of the drink. "But I can always make more."

"This is plenty," Ellen said. "We don't mean to be a bother."

"Are you kidding? I was thrilled when I read Sue's email this morning. I'm fascinated with this topic, and my friends and family are tired of me talking about it. It's nice to have some fresh ears."

"We're looking for a possible connection between the victims," Sue explained. "What can you tell us about the members of your family that killed themselves on Suicide Bridge?"

"Good luck with that," Teresa said. "Other than the family connections, they don't have much in common. Let's see. My Uncle Regis and Cousin Diego were both in the health field. My Aunt Cindy and Aunt Carla were homemakers. Cindy did some sewing for people, but she was mostly a stay-at-home mom, like Carla."

"Were they all born here in Santa Fe?" Tanya asked.

"Yes. And that's true of all of the victims."

"So that's another common denominator other than family connections," Sue pointed out. "What about hobbies or activities?"

"They participated in Fiesta de Santa Fe," she said, "though that's not true of many of the other victims. My uncle and cousin fished a lot. Cindy hated to fish. She and Carly were crafty. They dabbled in pottery."

"This isn't going to be easy," Ellen said.

"What about their common ancestors?" Tanya asked. "Do you know anything about the first Castillos that settled here?"

"They were Spanish conquistadors," Teresa said. "My oldest ancestor took part in reclaiming New Mexico from the Indians in 1692. Many of my ancestors fought in wars. My great-great grandfather died fighting in the Mexican American War in 1848. And my great-grandfather, Rudy, was one of the New Mexico National Guard that became part of the 200th regiment in World War II. He was proud to have been one of the Battling Bastards of Bataan."

"Were the victims at Suicide Bridge related to these war heroes?" Ellen asked.

"I don't know about the other victims, but the Castillos were."

"Wait a minute," Tanya said, her eyes beaming. "The Battle of Bataan—the Bataan Death March. Dave always talks about this. The Japanese were brutal to the Americans they captured in Bataan."

"Many of those prisoners were from Santa Fe, including my grandfather," Teresa said.

The wheels of Ellen's mind began to spin. If the Shinigami was Japanese, there might be a connection.

Ellen leaned forward. "Do you know if any of the other suicide victims had ancestors that fought in the Pacific War?"

"It never occurred to me to ask. I don't understand your line of reasoning."

Sue cleared her throat. "We're paranormal investigators, and we believe there may be some kind of spiritual warfare involved."

Ellen nodded. "We suspect a vengeful spirit may have targeted the victims for a specific reason."

Teresa scratched her head and frowned. "This is way out of my league. I don't know anything about the paranormal. I'm not even sure if I believe in it."

"That's okay. We understand," Tanya said. "Not everybody does."

"My parents and older brother believe in that stuff," she added. "They're obsessed with their religion. But my younger brother and I went a different way."

"Do you know how to get in touch with the families of some of the other victims?" Sue asked.

"I have email addresses. I can send them to you."

"That would be very helpful," Sue said. "Thank you."

"We used to have a large group of veterans that were prisoners of war together in Bataan," Teresa said. "They're all dead now. A lot of them participated in the protests against the Japanese American Internment Camp Memorial over at Frank S. Ortiz Dog Park. My grandfather was one of them. My father is still upset over it."

Ellen gasped. "Internment camp?"

"Oh, yes. From 1942 through 1946, an internment camp existed where the Casa Solana Subdivision is now. Japanese Americans, mainly from the west coast, were taken from their homes and put in ten different camps. The Santa Fe camp was one of the largest and housed men that were considered dangerous."

"Casa Solana?" Ellen's throat went dry. "That's where my fixer upper is located."

Sue and Tanya raised their brows.

"Did your grandfather ever visit the internment camp?" Ellen asked.

"Yes, he did. Not long after he returned from the war, he and a group of others who'd been prisoners of war went to vent, I guess you would say."

They talked for a little while longer, and then Ellen and her friends thanked the young woman for her time before heading back to La Fonda.

Later, while they were lunching back at the hotel, Sue announced that Lizzy Little had replied to her email. Lizzy had a shop on Canyon Road—a pottery shop called Lizzy's Lizards. She invited them to stop by any time.

"That was quick," Ellen said, since Sue had only just emailed the suicide victims' families when they were seated at their table.

They took the rental over to Canyon Road, passing Angie's Gallery and the corner café where they'd visited with Darren Cole the previous day. Lizzy's Lizards was a colorful studio filled with pottery of all kinds—platters, mugs, vases, goblets, wall art, figurines, and garden décor featuring desert animals, especially lizards. As they entered the studio, a short plump woman wearing an orange and green apron greeted them inside the door with a big smile. She had short brown hair, long eyelashes, and thick lips.

"Welcome to Lizzy's Lizards. How can I help you?"

"I'm Sue, and these are my friends Ellen and Tanya."

"The paranormal investigators?"

"Yes, that's right," Ellen said.

"Thanks for agreeing to meet with us," Tanya added.

"I'm not sure how much help I can be. I didn't know the Littles who died on Suicide Bridge very well."

"That's okay," Sue said. "We were wondering if they may have shared a common ancestor that was involved in the Pacific War."

Lizzy put a hand on one hip. "My great-grandfather was a Navajo code talker. Chayton Little. He was their ancestor, too."

"A Navajo what?" Sue asked.

"Code talker," Lizzy repeated. "He was a Navajo marine who helped to develop and utilize a secret code based on the language of the Navajo people. It was the only code the Axis forces couldn't break during World War II."

"How interesting," Ellen said. "But I don't suppose he or any of your other ancestors had anything to do with the Japanese American internment camp that used to be here back then."

"His best friend was a guard there," Lizzy offered. "I think he played baseball with the guards against the inmates."

They chatted with Lizzy for another half hour, but she provided little else about the suicide victims from the Little family. Sue bought a pair of clay lizard earrings for her daughter Lexi, and then the three friends shopped along Canyon Road for a couple of hours.

As they were returning to the rental, Sue said, "We should ask Darren Cole if the West family had relatives involved in the Pacific War."

"Good idea," Tanya said. "Angie's Gallery is only a block from here. Should we walk over there?"

"Sure," Ellen said.

Monica greeted them from behind the counter as soon as they walked in. Darren wasn't with her today.

They exchanged pleasantries, and then Sue asked how well she knew the West family.

"Angie was one of my best friends," Monica said. "I knew them fairly well. Why?"

Ellen explained their theory about the victims having ancestors related to the Pacific War, and, more specifically, to the Japanese American internment camp in Santa Fe.

"Jay West was a guard at the camp," Monica said. "He was an art-ist—an illustrator. You can find his work in the Collections from the Pacific War at the New Mexico History Museum near the plaza."

"Thank you so much," Ellen said.

As they returned to the rental, Ellen asked, "Do you think it's possi-ble that Jay West was Lizzy Little's ancestor's friend?"

"I'll give her a call," Sue said.

"Should we visit the museum this afternoon and take a look at his drawings?" Tanya asked.

"I'm game," Ellen said.

Sue frowned. "My feet hurt. Why don't you two go and let me know if you learn anything."

Ellen parked the car at La Fonda, and then she and Tanya walked a couple of blocks to the museum while Sue returned to her room to rest. Although the illustrations were interesting, they mainly depicted bored guards in humorous positions: one sat picking his teeth, another swatted at flies as he read a book, another sat at a desk doodling. If the illustra-tions represented what guard life was really like at the camp, it seemed to Ellen that not much went on.

Only one illustration by West suggested violence. Three little boys on the outside of a tall barbed-wire fence threw rocks at an old Japanese American who walked with a cane. The piece possessed the same de-spondent tone of boredom, but it was much darker than the others. West's sympathies were clearly with the old man, whose head was bleed-ing.

They scanned the other art in the museum, and near the end of the exhibit Tanya beckoned to Ellen, who was a few paces behind her.

"Look over here," Tanya said. "This artist is Ben Nishimura. It's a painting of the internment camp."

It was called *Funeral for Dr. Sadakazu Furugochi*, and, according to the plaque beneath the painting, it depicted a crowd of prisoners wearing identification numbers on their jackets gathered before a closed casket, a

Shinto priest, and a Christian minister. They were surrounded by a tall barbed-wire fence, a menacing guard tower, and the Sangre de Cristo Mountains.

Ellen smiled at Tanya. "You know what this means, don't you?"

"The key to helping the trapped souls is this internment camp," Tanya said.

"Yes," Ellen said. "And the next thing we need to do is to make contact with the Shinigami."

"You can't be serious," Tanya said.

"I am serious. We can't help the suicide victims move on until we help this vengeful spirit to find peace. Maybe the priest can help."

"Hmm. I'm not so sure about this next step of yours. Let's proceed with caution."

As they walked back to La Fonda, Ellen texted Sue: *We got a lead in the case.*

Sue replied: *So did I. Come to my room asap.*

CHAPTER NINE

Ben Nishimura

Ellen woke up Monday morning after another strange dream eager to begin the day. Throughout the night, the old Japanese woman had followed Ellen everywhere she went. The woman had asked, "Is he here? I thought he was here?" Ellen wondered if the woman was related to the shade of Santa Fe.

Before bed, Ellen and her friends had made appointments to speak with three people with promising leads in their case. While the artist, Ben Nishimura, a Japanese American in his sixties, was unavailable to meet in person, he'd agreed to a phone conference Monday morning at nine o'clock. Father Yamamoto had confirmed their appointment at 2:00 to discuss the Shinigami. And Sue's lead, a local paranormal investigator named Jane Connor, had invited Ellen and her friends to her lab that evening at 7:00 P.M.

Sue had also confirmed that Lizzy Little's ancestor's friend was indeed the guard and illustrator, Jay West. Ellen was excited that the pieces of the puzzle were coming together.

The restaurant downstairs in the La Fonda was less crowded this morning as the three friends made their way to a quiet booth. While they drank coffee and ate their breakfast, they discussed the questions they needed to ask the artist. When nine o'clock approached, Ellen stared at her phone, anticipating Ben Nishimura's call.

At five minutes past nine, Tanya said, "I hope he didn't forget us."

"Maybe I should call him," Ellen suggested.

"Golly. It's only been five minutes," Sue complained. "And he specifically said that he'd call us."

"That's true," Tanya said. "He said he'd be on the road, didn't he?"

"Yes," Sue said. "Travelling out of town for an art show or something."

Ellen took a sip of her coffee. The waitress arrived to clear their plates. Just as the waitress was asking if she could get them anything else, Ellen's phone rang.

"It's him!" Ellen said.

To the waitress, Sue said, "No thank you," as Ellen answered the call and put the phone on speaker.

"Hello, Mr. Nishimura," Ellen said. "Thank you so much for agreeing to speak with us."

"Sorry I'm running late this morning," he said.

"No worries." Sue glared at her friends. "We're just grateful you could talk to us at all."

"We're interested to hear everything you know about the Japanese American internment camp that was located in Santa Fe," Tanya said.

"Everything I know?" he repeated. "That could take quite a while."

"We'd be grateful for any time you can give us," Ellen said.

"There's a book my cousin co-authored," he said. "You might want to get a copy. It's called *Silent Voices of World War II: When Sons of the Land of Enchantment Met Sons of the Land of the Rising Sun.*"

"Write that down," Sue said to Ellen.

Ellen wasn't sure why Sue didn't just write it down herself, but she said nothing as she grabbed a pen and note pad from her purse and made a note of the book's title.

"Wonderful," Tanya said. "Thanks so much. We'll definitely buy the book."

"Something my cousin wrote in it, and something I agree with, is the great irony of World War II," the artist said. "We were fighting to put an end to Hitler's concentration camps, the cruel German regime, and the horrible treatment of conquered people, and in the process of doing that, the United States did the very thing it was fighting to prevent. Isn't that ironic? Over 120,000 Japanese Americans were interned during the war. I think Americans were reacting to the attack on Pearl Harbor, even though a study conducted by the U.S. government proved that no Japanese Americans were involved with that attack. And a report conducted prior to the attack—the Munson report—concluded that Japanese Americans were loyal to America. But I guess the politicians didn't read the reports. Or maybe their fear overcame their sense of logic."

"I didn't know about those reports," Ellen said. "That kind of puts things into perspective, doesn't it?"

"It just proves how unnecessary these camps were," Ben said. "Some people said it was to protect the Japanese Americans from civilian hate crimes, but the cost wasn't worth such protection. And the cost wasn't just in dollars. Families and individuals went through unnecessary suffering and loss. Some of the people who were loyal to America felt betrayed and realigned themselves with Japan. Their U.S. citizenship was revoked. Did you know that? They became people without a country. And then, before it was decided where they would be relocated, the Japanese Americans were asked two questions that were impossible to answer. I mean, they were damned no matter what they said."

"What were the questions?" Sue asked.

"Each man over the age of seventeen was asked if he was willing to serve in the U.S. armed forces on combat duty. He was also asked if he would swear unqualified allegiance to the United States and foreswear any allegiance or obedience to imperial Japan."

Tanya furrowed her brows. "How were those impossible questions?"

"If their American citizenship hadn't been revoked, they would have been easier to answer," Ben explained. "But now they had to think about what would happen to them if they became prisoners of war. Would the U.S. fight for their freedom, even though they weren't U.S.

citizens? Or would they be considered expendable casualties of war? And how would imperial Japan treat them? As men without a country, would the treatment of prisoners established by the Geneva Convention apply to them? And, if Japan were to win the war and learn that they'd betrayed their emperor, what fate would befall them and their families without an American citizenship to protect them?"

"I see," Ellen said. "Now I know what you mean about them being impossible to answer."

"But they had to answer them," the artist continued. "Those who said yes were put into camps with their families, and many of them were recruited to fight in the war. Those who said no or who qualified their answers by insisting that their citizenship be reinstated and their constitutional rights be protected were considered dangerous aliens. They were taken from their families and put into men-only camps, including the one in Santa Fe."

"How awful," Tanya said. "They were only trying to protect themselves. They weren't necessarily trying to be disloyal to America."

"Exactly," Ben said. "But you can bet that their feelings of loyalty changed after the way their country treated them. Many remained loyal despite everything, but a lot of them became loyal to Japan. A lot of them returned to Japan after the war, fed up with America."

"But not your ancestors," Sue said. "They stayed. Or you wouldn't be here."

"True."

"Why did they stay?" Tanya asked.

"First, you need to understand the difference between Issei, Nisei, and Sansei," Ben said. "The Issei were of the oldest generation. They were born in Japan and immigrated to America and had begun to build a life here. Many of them became citizens but not all, mainly because of difficult immigration laws. And most of them still had family ties to Japan, spoke Japanese, and lived the Japanese culture. My great-grandparents, Kiyoshi and Aiya, were Issei. Next were the Nisei. They were born in America. Most of them were taught the Japanese language and culture at home though they were educated in the United States. They were all American citizens but had warm feelings about their Japanese culture. My grandparents, Ren and Cho, were Nisei. Then there were those of the youngest generation, the Sansei. These were the children of the Nisei. Most of these were children who didn't know how to speak Japanese and didn't know much about their culture. They didn't feel any connection to Japan. They were fully assimilated into American life. My father, Benjiro, and uncle, Yamato, were Sansei. They were aged five and four. All three types were put into concentration camps. To the U.S. officials, they were all the same. They were 'Japs.' My grandfather told me that there was a sign on a storefront near where they lived in Los Angeles before relocation. It read 'Jap Hunting Licenses Issued Here. Open Season—No Limit.'"

"How awful!" Tanya cried again. "I'm so sorry they had to live through that."

"The sign was just one example of the extreme racial hatred expressed by other Americans toward Japanese Americans, and it wasn't the worst thing my ancestors had to live through. The worst was being separated from one another for over four years. My father had no contact with his father or grandfather during that time, except for a few letters. It was very hard on him and on the entire family. They were also worried for my father's uncle who was serving in the U.S. military. He had answered yes to the two impossible questions and was killed in combat just weeks before the end of the war."

"I can only imagine how hard that was for your family," Ellen said with a shake of her head.

"It was very hard. My grandmother and her mother-in-law lived with my father and uncle in a tiny one-room barrack at a camp in Wyoming where they were served a gross dish that the Americans called 'Slop-Suey.' My ancestors nearly froze to death during the winters, which often reached 35 degrees below zero."

"Didn't they have heat?" Tanya asked.

"A very primitive potbelly stove. My grandmother, Cho, had to scavenge for lumber scraps to keep the fire going."

Ellen shook her head again. "Unbelievable."

"The Japanese culture teaches its people to avoid shame," Ben continued. "Being treated in such disrespectful ways by U.S. officials brought immense shame upon my ancestors and their fellow Japanese Americans. The psychological toll was even greater than the physical. Then there was the financial toll. My great-grandfather owned a shop in Los Angeles. He had grown wealthy but lost everything when he was interned. My grandfather was a journalist for a Japanese language newspaper and a translator at his church. My grandmother was a secretary at the same church. Both lost their jobs. It only added to their feelings of shame."

"What was it like for your grandfather and great-grandfather at the camp in Santa Fe?" Sue asked.

"Boring. Because they were essentially prisoners of war, the rules of the Geneva Convention prevented them from being put to work. They weren't used to this. They were hard-working men that often worked on the weekends, too. They were sick with boredom. My grandfather wrote in a letter to my grandmother that he wanted to live in a house without locks or without doors because being imprisoned was killing his soul. He and my great-grandfather, along with some of the other prisoners, grew vegetables in front of their barracks. They did this because they despised the food that they were served in the mess hall and because they needed something to make the dreary days go by faster. They were so successful that the guards allowed them to create a poultry farm and to prepare their own food. This improved their lives dramatically. My grandfather, Ren, started a camp newspaper and recruited other prisoners to get involved. This also gave them something to do and helped uplift their morale. They were fortunate to have guards who allowed these things."

"Did your ancestors tell you about any noteworthy occasions of violence or murder at the camp?" Ellen asked.

"There were two riots," Ben said. "One happened right after the Bataan Death March. The citizens were outraged by the reports of how American prisoners of war were treated by the Japanese. An angry mob went to the barbed wire fence of the camp armed with hatchets and shotguns. They didn't shoot, but they threw rocks, spit, shouted, and basically took out their anger on the interned—who of course had nothing to do with what had happened in Bataan. The camp officials convinced the mob that their actions might backfire on their loved ones imprisoned in Japan, so the mob dispersed after fifteen minutes."

"And the other incident?" Tanya asked.

"There was a subgroup of the Nisei called Kibei. They were born in America but returned to Japan for part of their education before coming back to America. They resented the way they were being treated by the U.S., and a group of them that had been interned at another camp renounced their loyalty to America. Over 300 of them were eventually transferred to Santa Fe, where they tried to drum up support from the other prisoners for their subversive plans. When they didn't get it, they used death threats and violence. They made the camp a living hell for my grandfather and great-grandfather and the other prisoners. And then in March of 1945, things erupted. The camp officials were transferring a couple of the troublemakers back to a different camp when about 200 prisoners protested with violence. My great-grandfather was mistaken for one of the troublemakers and was beaten so severely that he had to be hospitalized for a week. After that, my grandfather, Ren, was tempted to renounce his loyalty to the U.S., but after Kiyoshi became severely ill and Ren was allowed to work as an orderly in the hospital so he could be close to his father, he changed his mind. He decided that the U.S. had a heart after all."

"What happened to them after the war?" Sue asked.

"They were reunited with the rest of their family. Because Kiyoshi was so ill and hospitalized, they, unlike many of the prisoners, stayed in Santa Fe and started a new life there. Ren continued to work as an orderly. He bought a modest home for the rest of his family and built a garden and chicken coop. Later, after his father died, he left his job at the hospital and became a journalist for the local newspaper. My father also became a journalist and later met and married my mother, an artist. My uncle became a gardener, so, in a sense, they each followed in their father's footsteps. Life went on, you know?"

"I'm glad your story had a happy ending," Sue said, "but I have another question that isn't very happy. You see, we're paranormal investigators trying to help the tethered souls of the victims of Suicide Bridge. We've been told that six of those victims shared the name Nishimura. Were they relatives of yours?"

"Yes. My uncle, four cousins, and my daughter."

"I'm so sorry to hear that, especially that one was your daughter," Tanya said. "I can imagine no worse pain than losing a child."

"Neither can I," Ben said. "It happened over twenty years ago, but the loss still feels fresh. It devastated my marriage. When our son turned eighteen, twelve years ago, my wife and I finally went our separate ways."

"I'm so sorry," Ellen said.

"Did your daughter suffer from depression?" Sue asked.

"That's the only explanation for what happened," Ben said. "None of us knew it at the time, though. Maybe if we had…"

"There might be another explanation," Ellen said. "You see, a priest in Santa Fe saw a Shinigami on my head. He quickly rebaptized me to get rid of it. In our investigation into the victims of Suicide Bridge, we've found that many seem to have ancestors connected to the internment camp that was located here in Santa Fe."

"We believe that the Shinigami might be responsible for the deaths at Suicide Bridge," Sue added, "and we're wondering if, in any of the stories you were told, there was ever mention of someone who died at the camp who may have become a vengeful spirit."

"I'm sorry, but I don't believe in any of that nonsense. Shinigami are creatures of mythology."

Ellen felt the blood rush to her face. "We understand. It wasn't that long ago that I felt the same way as you."

"We thank you for your time, Mr. Nishimura," Sue said. "And we hope we haven't upset you by asking you to recall unhappy memories."

"Yes," Tanya chimed in. "Thank you so much."

"A day doesn't go by that I don't recall them," he said. "I'm glad I could be of help to you."

When the call had ended, Ellen looked at her friends and sighed. "Well, that was certainly insightful. It explains why we are dealing with a vengeful spirit."

"We just need to find out his identity," Sue said. "I wonder how many prisoners died while they were interned at the camp here in Santa Fe."

"There must be records, don't you think?" Tanya said.

"I'm sure," Sue agreed. "Why don't we go back to my room and conduct some more research until it's time to meet the priest?"

"Let's go," Ellen said.

CHAPTER TEN

Rosario Cemetery

B ack in Sue's hotel room, the three friends got busy trying to find the names of any internees who died at the Santa Fe camp. Ellen scanned through one article after another, but most of them focused on the riot that Ben Nishimura had told them about. Discouraged, Ellen took a break to get a bucket of ice and a Diet Coke from the vending room down the hall. When she returned, Sue had found something.

"I discovered a page from an online book called *Confinement and Ethnicity: An Overview of World War II Japanese American Relocation Sites.* Listen to this paragraph: *After the end of the war the Santa Fe facility was used as a holding and processing center for other internment camps. As late as March 1946, 200 Japanese American men were transferred to Santa Fe from Fort Lincoln. However, by May only 12 of these remained. The camp closed shortly thereafter, and all property was sold as surplus (Thomas et al. 1994). Today the camp site is within a residential subdivision. At the Rosario Cemetery, -1/2 mile east of the camp site, there are graves from two Japanese American men who died during the internment (Narvot 1999a). A State History Museum committee has proposed placing a plaque paid for with private funds at Frank Ortiz City Park overlooking the site, but as of 1999 local opposition has delayed the plaque's installation (Narvot 1999b)."*

"Should we visit the Rosario Cemetery and look for them?" Ellen asked.

"I wouldn't mind stretching my legs," Tanya said.

"Who doesn't love a stroll in a cemetery?" Sue said sarcastically. "But might I recommend that we call the office? We don't have the names of the deceased, and there could be hundreds of graves with Japanese names."

"I doubt there are hundreds," Ellen said as she cracked open her Diet Coke, "but calling them is a good idea. Why don't you do the honors?"

Less than an hour later, Ellen and her friends were driving toward the location given to them by the cemetery staff. They had been told that two Japanese Americans from the internment camp were buried in 1945 in the northern part of the cemetery known as the Rose Garden. The names of the men were Nobuyoshi Sudo and Gentaro Yoshikawa.

Ellen parked on the side of Rosario Street. They had been told to look for a rectangular plot that had only twenty graves—all old and badly worn. The plot would be directly south of a triangular plot and across the street from the Santa Fe National Cemetery.

The Rose Garden plot was not hard to find. A rectangle of dead grass without a single rose, it was the smallest section in the entire cemetery. The headstones of the two Japanese Americans were side by side.

As soon as Ellen stepped onto the dead grass, an uneasy feeling washed over her.

"I just got chills," Tanya said.

"I felt it, too," Sue said. "This is a feeling you don't get when you are surrounded by those at peace. It's unsettling."

"It is," Ellen agreed. "I think we might be onto something."

"Are you wearing your *gris gris*?" Tanya asked.

All three friends pulled out the leather cords they wore around their necks to show the small protective bags they'd bought from a Voodoo priestess in New Orleans.

Sue stood before the first of the two headstones. "N. Sudo, born July 23, 1884, died January 9, 1945."

"So, he was sixty when he died," Tanya said.

Ellen lifted her brows. "I'm impressed, Tanya. That was pretty fast math."

Tanya rolled her eyes.

"I wonder what those Japanese symbols mean," Sue said. "I'm going to snap a photo and see if Father Yamamoto can translate them."

"Good idea," Tanya said.

Ellen turned to the other grave and read, "D. Yoshikawa. I thought we were told his first name was Gentaro."

"We were," Sue said.

"Hmm. Maybe he went by another name," Ellen said. "He was born December 27, 1881 and died June 6, 1945.

"That would make him how old, Tanya?" Sue asked.

"Sixty-three."

Ellen remembered that she'd be turning sixty next year.

"We need to find out what killed them," Sue said. "The more we can learn about them, the better we'll be able to determine if either one of them might be our Shinigami."

Tanya pushed her blonde hair from her eyes. "Now that we have names and dates, that should be easier to do."

As they were about to return to the rental, Ellen felt something brush across her legs. She jumped about a foot into the air and then lost her balance and fell onto the dead grass, landing on her hip.

"Are you okay?" Sue asked as she offered Ellen a hand.

Ellen took Sue's hand and, climbing to her feet, said, "Something just brushed across my legs. At first, I thought it was a cat."

"Let's get out of here." Tanya hurried to the rental, leaving Sue and Ellen in her wake.

Later over lunch at a seafood restaurant across from the cemetery, Ellen and her friends compared notes from their internet research.

"I found an article that briefly mentions our two graves," Ellen said. "On a site called *Everyday Knosticism*, an article called 'Cemetery Tales' reports that Nobuyoshi Sudo was born in Japan and was a railyard worker in Louisiana when he was interned. The article says: *He left behind his American born wife, Zettie Isabella (née Stork) from Tennessee and two American born sons, 19-year-old Nile and 10-year-old Victor. So immersed was he in American culture that he chose to go by the name 'William' on his employment and Census records starting around 1930, and on his official naturalization papers—signed and approved just a few months before his arrest—on 13 January, 1942.*"

"How sad," Tanya cried. "He'd just become a citizen."

Sue took a sip of her Cherry Coke. "Does the article say what killed him?"

"No, it doesn't. That's all it says about that grave. It then goes on to say that the second grave belonged to Gentaro Yoshikawa, also born in Japan. He was a U.S. Naval laundry worker living in Vallejo, California when he was interned. He was arrested for possessing Navy signal flags, which he was laundering for his job. But he was arrested anyway. That's so unfair."

"Sounds like a vengeful spirit in the making, if you ask me," Sue said.

"Well, you might want to revise that theory after you hear this," Ellen said before taking another bite of her shrimp salad. "According to this article, at least forty-two Japanese American prisoners died while incarcerated at the Santa Fe camp."

"What happened to them? Why are only two buried at Rosario Cemetery?" Tanya wondered.

Sue cut a piece of fish and loaded it onto her fork. "They were probably sent to their family cemeteries."

"This article suggests that some of them could be buried in the same plot as the others in unmarked graves," Ellen said. "At the time, it was considered a potter's field of sorts."

"What's a potter's field?" Tanya asked before taking a drink of her water.

"That's what you call a burial ground where poor people and John Does and people without any family are buried," Sue explained.

"Ben Nishimura painted a funeral scene from the camp," Ellen said. "We should call him back and ask if he knows anything about the other prisoners who died there."

"Good idea," Sue said. "Let's do it."

Ellen made the call.

"Hello, Mrs. McManius," the artist said on the other line. "What can I do for you?"

"Please call me Ellen," she said. "I have you on speaker with Tanya and Sue. We have another question for you if you have a minute."

"As it happens, I have ten minutes. What's your question?"

Ellen leaned forward. "Do you know of any Japanese American prisoners who may have died at the camp and then were buried in unmarked graves?"

"Or what happened to the prisoners who died?" Sue asked. "Were their bodies sent home?"

"My grandfather told me that there was a place known as the pauper's field," Ben said. "It wasn't far from the camp. I don't know its exact location."

Ellen raised her brows and glanced at her friends.

Then Tanya asked, "Mr. Nishimura, do you know of any prisoners who may have been unjustly killed or murdered while living at the camp?"

There was a long silence on the other end. Ellen wondered if they'd lost their connection.

"Are you still there?" she asked.

"I'm here," the artist replied. "My grandfather told me a story that was supposed to remain a secret. If I tell it to you, I need your word that you won't print it or share it publicly."

"You have our word," Sue said as she glanced expectantly at Tanya and Ellen.

Ellen sat forward in her seat.

"Do you remember what I told you earlier about the Kibei that came to Santa Fe from another internment camp?"

"Yes?" Ellen said.

"They used death threats and violence to garner support from the original inmates, remember?"

"Yes," Ellen said again.

"Well, one of them, a man named Haruto Okada, threatened to kill my great-grandfather on the morning of the riot if he didn't pledge his loyalty to Japan. When Kiyoshi told Okada that he could go to hell, Okada, who was bigger and stronger, put my great-grandfather into a death grip, threatening to break his neck. My grandfather, fearing for his father's life, hid a rusty nail in his fist, with the sharp end out. He called Okada a coward for attacking an old man. Okada released Kiyoshi and charged Ren. Just as the prison riot broke out, my father plunged the nail into Okada's neck. Okada bled out. During the chaos, Kiyoshi and Ren hid Okada's body. Then Ren was mistaken for one of the rioters and was beaten by a guard who didn't know him. While Ren was recovering in the hospital, Kiyoshi confessed to one of the friendlier guards he'd known for a long time. After hearing Kiyoshi's story, the guard enlisted the help of a few local friends, and, together with Kiyoshi, they secretly buried the body in the pauper's field."

"You wouldn't happen to know the names of the men who helped Kiyoshi to bury Okada?" Ellen asked.

"The guard was the famous illustrator, Jay West," Ben said. "And his friends were named Rudy Castillo, Chuck Jensen, and Chayton Little."

Ellen gasped.

"Thank you, Mr. Nishimura," Sue said. "You've been a great help to us. I hope you enjoy the rest of your trip."

After they ended the call, the three friends sat together processing what they'd just discovered. Many of the victims of Suicide Bridge were descendants of the men who secretly buried Haruto Okada in the pauper's field. Could Haruto Okada be the Shinigami?

Ellen did a quick Google search on her phone.

"Listen to this," she said after she'd clicked on an article in her search results. "One Japanese American family's search for a relative interned during World War II continues decades after the man went missing in 1946. After the attack on Pearl Harbor, Haruto Okada, who had been serving in the U.S. Army, was reclassified as a dangerous alien. He was relocated to three different camps from 1942-1945, but inconsistencies in the official records have added to the difficulty in locating his remains. It is unknown whether Okada died while he was interned, and, if so, at which camp, or if he died sometime after release."

"We need to help that family," Tanya said. "If Haruto Okada is buried in an unmarked grave in the Rose Garden section at Rosario Cemetery, they can finally have the answers they've been looking for."

CHAPTER ELEVEN

Father Yamamoto

The rectory beside the Cathedral Basilica of St. Francis of Assisi was a modest adobe building with two floors and lots of windows. Father Yamamoto was waiting for Ellen, Sue, and Tanya in the lobby. He jumped up from a wooden chair and rushed to the door to greet them as they entered.

The priest wore his black hair cut short, with bangs reaching his thin, dark brows. Wrinkles appeared around the corners of his black eyes when he smiled. He was nearly as short as Sue and was thin and wiry beneath his black cassock.

"It's good to see you without that thing on your head," he said to Ellen as he took her hand in both of his and gave it a squeeze. "I imagine it's even better for you than it is for me."

"I do feel lighter," Ellen said with a grin.

As he greeted Tanya and Sue in the same fashion, he added, "I made you each a bottle of holy water in case he comes back. It's over there on the table. Please, have a seat."

He motioned to the sitting area around a coffee table, where three plastic bottles marked *Holy Water* were sitting.

"Thank you," Tanya said. "That was nice of you."

"You know how we make this stuff, don't you?" he asked.

"You bless it?" Sue asked.

"We boil the Hell out of it," he said with a laugh.

Ellen chuckled at the priest's joke as she took her seat beside Tanya on a wooden bench with upholstered cushions. The room was warm, and she felt a hot flash coming on.

Sue sat in a chair adjacent to the priest. "We can't thank you enough for being our knight in shining armor last Sunday."

"I was glad to be of service," he said.

"We're anxious to learn what you know about Shinigami," Ellen said, leaning forward in her seat. "We've been conducting some research and have discovered some interesting things on our own."

"Oh? Would you mind sharing them with me?"

Ellen and her friends told the priest about the victims of Suicide Bridge and what many of them seemed to have in common—ancestors who were present at the secret burial of a Kibei rebel who was killed at the Santa Fe internment camp. They told him that Haruto Okada's family had been searching for his remains for decades.

"We think he's buried at Rosario Cemetery," Sue said.

"Show him the photos," Tanya said. "Maybe he can translate the characters."

"Oh, right," Sue pulled up the photos she had taken at the cemetery on her phone and showed them to the priest. "Do you know what those Japanese characters say?"

"Beloved son, husband, and father," he read. "The second one says beloved son and brave soldier."

Ellen wondered what would have been written on Haruto Okada's grave.

"I'm impressed with how quickly you were able to formulate this theory," Father Yamamoto said.

"Our hope is to bring peace to the Shinigami," Ellen explained, "so that we can then help the souls who died at Suicide Bridge to cross over."

"That's a noble plan," the priest said as he scratched his head. "But I've never known a Shinigami to be saved. And I've encountered many, to be sure."

"What kind of encounters have you had?" Sue asked.

"Since I was a young boy, I could see ghosts," he said. "I didn't know much about them then. Some were nice to me, some were indifferent, and others were cruel. The cruel ones frightened me."

"What did your parents think about your ability?" Tanya asked. "Did you tell them about it?"

"I come from a very religious family. They believed me and were frightened for me. They sent me to Catholic school and encouraged me to become a priest, believing that holy orders would protect me from what we call Shinigami. That's the name for the cruel ghosts."

"How did you know I was possessed by a cruel ghost and not one of the others?" Ellen asked.

"Firstly, you weren't possessed," the priest clarified. "The Shinigami was merely attached to you. Had he possessed you, a baptism may not have been enough to save you."

Ellen felt the color leave her face. She wiped away the beads of sweat that had formed on her forehead.

"Secondly, I knew it was a Shinigami because only cruel spirits attempt to feed off of the living."

"Cruel or desperate," Tanya said. "I had a spirit attachment a few years ago. The soul wasn't cruel per se."

Father Yamamoto cocked his head to the side. "Really? How do you know?"

Ellen and her friends told him about their experiences in New Orleans.

"How fascinating," he said. "I saw a red orb over your head, Ellen."

"We saw a red orb, too," Sue chimed in. "On our video, but not in person."

The priest nodded. "Had he not been attached to someone, I would have seen his human form. Usually they are shadow-like or have a gray pallor and often have red eyes."

"I saw his human form at Meow Wolf," Ellen said, "but only his reflection. And he did have red eyes."

"From what I've learned, a Shinigami wants one thing: to kill. He or she wants to induce more death and pain on the living. They usually dwell near areas where horrific deaths have occurred. Places of impurity where injustices have taken place attract the Shinigami. They prey on people who are themselves impure or who visit these places of impurity. This explains why deaths often happen in the same places over and over. A Shinigami is at work. Suicide Bridge is a prime example."

Ellen glanced nervously at her friends as goosebumps appeared on her arms. She'd just been sweating with a hot flash, and now she had chills.

"Do you know how the Shinigami gets people to kill themselves?" Sue asked.

"It will take possession of a person and force that person to become obsessed with everything bad they have done or with everything tragic they have experienced, driving that person to want to die."

Ellen shuddered.

Father Yamamoto sat back in his chair. "Such a place like Suicide Bridge must be purified to diminish the Shinigami's power."

"That's what we hope to do," Tanya said. "We want to purify the place and bring peace to the victims, so they can move on."

"It won't be easy," Father Yamamoto said with a shake of his head. "Shinigami are powerful creatures, unlike most ghosts."

"How do they get their power?" Sue asked.

"Their anger, their evil, it multiplies along with their power with the deaths of each of their victims."

"We have to do something, don't we, Father?" Ellen rubbed her temple.

"As I said, what you want to do is noble, but it is also dangerous. In my role as a priest, I have exorcized dozens of Shinigami from their victims. I failed once. It ended in a woman's death."

"What happened?" Sue asked. "Are you sure she was possessed and not ill?"

"You can tell the difference," Father Yamamoto said with a nod. "The victim's personality changes drastically. They usually growl and snarl in a voice different from their own. They also harm themselves by pulling out clumps of their hair or by cutting into their skin with their own fingernails or teeth."

"That sounds terrifying," Ellen said as a chill crawled down her spine.

"They also refer to themselves in the third person," he said. "They say things like, 'The devil wants Agatha. You cannot save her from him.'"

Tanya's face had become as white as a sheet. "This is scary stuff."

"Very scary," the priest said. "The woman who died had been a member of my parish in San Francisco for many years. She would never raise her voice, not even when her children were misbehaving. But once the Shinigami took possession of her, all that changed. She nearly killed her youngest son when she beat him with a baseball bat."

"Oh my God!" Sue cried.

"Her husband tried to stop her. He said she had overpowered him. When he called me for help, I brought three strong men to help me bind her to her bed."

"It took that much strength to overpower her?" Ellen asked in awe.

"Oh, yes. She hissed and snarled and growled and laughed at me. She told me Vilma was gone—that was her name—and that there was no saving her now. When I anointed her forehead with holy water, a rash appeared, and soon a boil. When I burned incense of sage and frankincense and myrrh, she began to vomit profusely, showering it across the room and all over me."

"What did you do?" Tanya asked.

"I stayed and prayed over her, attempting to banish the Shinigami from her body. When there was nothing left for her to vomit, I thought she was improving. But then I became aware of her shallow breathing. Soon after, her body shut down, and she stopped breathing altogether."

Ellen covered her mouth and held her breath, trying to process the priest's story.

"I was nearly indicted for murder," he added. "Fortunately, the coroner concluded that Vilma's death was from natural causes. But there was nothing natural about it."

"I've never heard of anything so frightening," Tanya said, visibly shaken.

"What happens to the Shinigami once it is exorcised?" Sue asked.

Father Yamamoto shrugged. "It moves on in search of other victims, I suppose."

"Is there no way to stop it?" Ellen wondered. "Have you ever tried?"

"I've heard of others using techniques to trap a Shinigami, but I never learned to do it myself."

"Maybe we shouldn't get involved," Tanya said. "This Shinigami could be out of our league."

"We can't just turn our backs on the souls at Suicide Bridge," Sue pointed out.

"You're right," Tanya admitted. "I know you're right."

"You'll need help," Father Yamamoto said. "And I'll do everything in my power to help you."

Ellen lifted her brows. "You will? You'll help us?"

"Of course," he said. "I like the idea of trying to save the Shinigami and would be interested to see if it can be done. I would also like to recruit the help of one of my colleagues, who is currently in San Francisco. Perhaps I can convince him to come for a visit."

"We would be so grateful," Ellen said.

Tanya didn't look as excited as Ellen felt.

"Tanya? Are you okay?"

Tanya shrugged. "I'm just wondering what the heck we've gotten ourselves into this time."

"We'll be careful," Ellen reassured her. "I promise."

"We're meeting a paranormal investigator this evening at 7 p.m.," Sue said to the priest. "She's an expert at clearing negative energy. Would you like to join us?"

"Is it Jane Connor?" he asked.

Ellen lifted her chin. "You know her?"

"Oh, yes. We've worked together many times with some local problems. I wish I could join you this evening, but I have a rosary to lead. One of my parishioners passed last week."

"I'm sorry to hear that," Sue said.

"Thank you," Father Yamamoto said. "If you give me enough advance warning, I can make sure to be there when you're ready to face the Shinigami."

Ellen and her friends stood up.

"Thank you, Father," Ellen said. "We'll be in touch."

CHAPTER TWELVE

The Local Paranormal Investigator

That evening after dinner, Ellen, Sue, and Tanya met Jane Connor at her lab ten minutes away from their hotel on Cerrillos Road. The lab was in a strip mall, and, from the outside, it looked more like an office than a lab. It had an insurance company on one side of it and a yogurt shop on the other. But once they stepped inside, Ellen recognized many of the same instruments they used in their own investigations.

"Hello," a woman said from the back of the room. She was a petite woman in her sixties with reddish brown hair that fell in bangs down to her black-rimmed glasses. Her blouse, trousers, and flats were black, too. "Welcome to Connor Energy Clearing Services. I'm Jane. Is one of you Sue?"

Sue waved. "That's me. Hi, Jane. These are my friends, Ellen and Tanya."

"Thanks so much for agreeing to meet with us," Ellen said.

"Of course," Jane said. "Please have a seat, and welcome to my lab-slash-studio-slash-office. I like to conduct my work away from home to keep my house clean, if you know what I mean."

"We do," Tanya said. "Believe me."

Behind Jane was a green screen flanked by two large studio lights. A camera on a tripod stood facing her from across the room, and behind it were shelves of various objects that gave Ellen the creeps. There were dolls, a clown head, a stack of old books, a small chest, an antique Tiffany lamp, and a Fabergé egg. Closer to the entrance were long tables with instruments that Ellen recognized as tools of the trade—EMF detectors, full spectrum cameras, an electromagnetic pump, ambient thermometers, EVP recorders, and a spirit box for picking up radio frequencies—a technique Ellen didn't have a lot of faith in but had been meaning to try, nevertheless. The fourth wall contained a large bookcase filled with books and a tall file cabinet.

Jane motioned to three office chairs that sat opposite her desk. As she took her own seat, she said, "I'm interested in learning what you've discovered so far. You know, I once tried to help the souls at Suicide Bridge, but it ended badly, and I haven't been back since."

"Really?" Ellen asked. "What happened?"

"Well, this was years ago, back when I was first getting started. Back then, I was still learning to have confidence in my abilities. It wasn't until I started working with a local priest who saw the same things I saw and could confirm that I wasn't imagining things that I began to have confidence."

"By any chance, was that Father Yamamoto?" Ellen asked.

"Yes. So, you've already met him?"

"He saw a Shinigami on my head and rebaptized me to get rid of it," Ellen explained.

"How fortunate for you that he caught it in time."

Ellen felt a chill slink down her spine.

"By the way, when I say I see things, I don't mean that I see them with my eyes," Jane said. "I see them with my mind's eye. Ever since I was a child, I saw ghosts this way."

Ellen wondered if that was true of her, too. Did she see ghosts with her eyes or with her mind's eye?

"It's taken me years to gain control over my abilities and to use them to help people. I clear residential and commercial properties of negative energy and have also performed exorcisms with Father Yamamoto. It was while I was clearing one of my very first homes that I met someone associated with Suicide Bridge. I had gone for an initial assessment—which I don't do anymore. Now I can clear properties without being on location. These days I do it on Zoom."

"Really?" Sue asked with a laugh. "That's incredible."

It seemed too incredible to Ellen, but she withheld her judgment. After all, Jane was offering them her help. Ellen was grateful for any direction the woman could offer.

"Anyway, I had gone for an initial assessment, and in the kitchen, I saw this tall, dark shade who was not happy to see me. There were other ghosts scurrying away from me as I entered, hiding behind doors and cabinets, but this particular ghost approached me and told me to get the F out."

"What did you do?" Tanya asked.

"I continued to assess the other rooms in the house, and then I left to come up with my plan," Jane said. "Something really interesting happened before my next visit. You see, the owner of the property, who was also astute and had experiences with the dead, had told everybody that I would be returning to send them home. It had never occurred to me to tell them that, but when I returned the next day, they were all lined up, waiting for me."

"They were eager to go home," Ellen said, "to cross to the other side."

Jane nodded. "Even the tall, dark shade from the kitchen was there, and he said to me, 'Welcome back, but I don't think you can help me. I don't know if I can find peace.' And I said, 'Why do you think that?' He said, 'I did a terrible thing. I was angry with my mother for not letting me be my own man. I felt trapped. And in a fit of rage, I grabbed the kitchen knife from this drawer, and I murdered her. I was sorry the in-stant I did it.'"

Tanya gasped. "What did you say to him? Were you able to help him?"

"Honestly, I didn't think I would be able to help him, but to my great surprise a woman I hadn't seen before appeared. The tall, dark shade said, 'Mom?' The woman put her arms around her son and helped him to the other side."

Chills tickled Ellen's neck, and goosebumps appeared on her arms. "What a wonderful experience that must have been."

"Wow," Tanya agreed. "I love that story."

"It had a profound impact on me," Jane said. "It helped me to real-ize that there are people on the other side who can help those who are trapped to cross over, especially if they can offer forgiveness to those left behind."

"That is a touching story," Sue said. "But how does it relate to the ghosts at Suicide Bridge?"

"Well, when I told Linda, the homeowner, what had happened with the shade, she told me that she wondered if I might visit the bridge where her sister had committed suicide, to make sure that her sister had moved on. Linda had had reoccurring nightmares in which her sister begged her for help. So, I agreed to go with her to the bridge."

"How long ago was this?" Ellen asked.

"This must have been about ten years ago," Jane said. "We went dur-ing the day—I like to go during the day because there tends to be less activity."

"Really?" Sue asked. "We were taught to work at night, so we can better capture images and sounds on our instruments."

"If I'm investigating, absolutely. I go at night for that. But if I'm try-ing to send someone home, I like to do it during the day."

"That makes sense," Sue said.

"The first thing I do is let the ghosts know that I'm there to help, not to harm. Then I ask for those on the other side who love this person to welcome them home with loving arms, without judgment. I also call upon angels to help. Usually someone, and sometimes many people, will come from the other side to usher their loved one home. But the day I went to the bridge and asked for help from the other side, no one came."

"No one?' Ellen asked. "Not even angels?"

Jane shook her head. "I tried to help Linda's sister on my own, but she was too confused, and there were others there that seemed to be holding her back."

"They don't understand what has happened to them," Sue said to Ellen and Tanya.

"Well, it was the one and only time in my career that I felt like a failure. I eventually accepted the fact that I can't always help. I do what I can, but that one time, it wasn't enough."

"What was Linda's sister's name?" Ellen asked.

"Barbara Jensen."

Ellen sucked in her lips and glanced at her friends. Jensen was the name of one of the men who had secretly buried Haruto Okada.

"We have a theory as to why you may not have been able to help," Sue said. "It has to do with the Shinigami Father Yamamoto saw on Ellen's head."

Ellen and her friends told Jane what they had learned, and, without telling her that Ben Nishimura's grandfather had killed Haruto Okada, they shared their theory that Okada was a Shinigami who had possessed the victims at Suicide Bridge.

"If they were possessed when they died, they may not even realize that they're dead," Ellen said. "If we explain what happened to them, and somehow stop the Shinigami from interfering with their attempts to cross over, then they may be able to move on."

"Do you know how to trap a Shinigami?" Tanya asked Jane.

Jane's brows lifted. "I know a method, but I've never attempted it. I feel that all ghosts should have the opportunity to be redeemed so they can move on."

"We feel the same way," Ellen said. "But we were thinking of trapping the Shinigami until we can set the victims of Suicide Bridge free. Then we'll turn our attention to helping him."

Jane nodded. "I like that idea. I'd be happy to help you in any way I can."

"Do we need any special instruments to trap one?" Tanya asked.

Jane leaned forward across her desk. "You need a compact mirror, at least two other mirrors, a bowl of holy water, and some duct tape."

CHAPTER THIRTEEN

New Discoveries

Tuesday morning, Ellen and her friends had just been seated in the restaurant at La Fonda for breakfast when the realtor called.

"Hi, Nancy," Ellen said into her phone.

"Hi, Ellen. Do you have time to come to the property this morning? The inspector has found something I think you'll want to see."

When Ellen relayed the news to her friends, they decided to postpone breakfast and drive over to the house on Luna Circle, where the inspector and Nancy were already waiting inside.

"Hello?" Ellen called as she entered the house, followed by Sue and Tanya.

"Hi, ladies," Nancy said as she emerged from the garage. "We're in here. Follow me."

Nancy led them into the garage, where the inspector stood with his flashlight. He had pulled the water heater out of its closet.

"This is Jonathon Rivers, the inspector," Nancy said.

He was a thin and wiry man in his late sixties with short white hair and a clean-shaven face.

"Hello," Ellen said. "What have you found?"

"It's a miracle I did find it," he said. "I almost didn't. I noticed that this water heater was sitting on what looked like a sheet of plywood. I thought what idiot would do such a thing and why wasn't the wood rotted. All water heaters leak eventually, especially in a house this old. So, I knocked on the wood to discover that it wasn't wood at all. It was a sheet of Formica."

"That's odd," Sue said.

"My thought exactly," Jonathon said. "I knocked again and heard it was hollow on the other side. I thought maybe more plumbing would be found beneath it. So, I pulled out the water heater to have a look and found this." He shined his light on the trapdoor, revealing a set of stone steps.

"What is it?" Ellen asked.

"A hidden cellar," he said. "Most likely a bomb shelter. Anyway, I found some interesting things inside. Care to follow me?"

Ellen turned on the flashlight on her phone and followed Jonathon down the steps into a cool, dark room that was about twenty feet wide and thirty feet deep. The ceiling was low—only about six or seven feet above the concrete floor. The walls were stone and mortar, and metal beams ran the length of the ceiling. There was an old round table and six chairs in one corner, a floor-to-ceiling metal shelving unit along the back wall, and four cots along a third wall.

Sue shined her light on the shelving unit and said, "Too bad it's not a wine cellar. That would have been a nice find."

"What is all this stuff?" Ellen wondered as she shined her light on the shelves.

"Maybe this will help," Jonathon said.

A humming noise filled the room, and less than a minute later, so did light.

"This is definitely a bomb shelter," Tanya said as she looked over the objects on the shelving unit. "Look at those oxygen tanks and all those canned goods. Someone expected to have to survive down here."

Jonathon nodded. "These bunkers aren't uncommon in New Mexico. After the Manhattan Project in Los Alamos became public, everyone in New Mexico wanted one. Nothing like having an atom bomb in your back yard to make you want to build an underground bunker."

"There's a bathroom behind this curtain," Nancy said from across the room. "A sink, toilet, and shower."

Ellen studied the objects on the shelves. On the top were folded blankets and pillows. At eye level were stacks of canned goods and rows of jarred preserves. She also saw jugs of water, a first aid kit, a toolbox, batteries, flashlights, a propane lantern and propane tank, propane cooking stove, eating utensils, bottles of iodine and potassium iodide, soap, and packages of toilet paper. On the bottom row of the shelving unit were books, magazines, board games, and several decks of cards. Whoever had stocked this place knew what they were doing.

"Check this out," Jonathon said. "A fireproof safe."

The safe was on the floor next to the shelving unit and stood about four feet high, two feet wide, and two feet deep. The door had a combination lock on it and a steel handle.

Ellen walked over to it and tried to open it, but it wouldn't budge. "I wonder what's in it. Is there a way to open it?"

"You can hire someone," Jonathon said. "You never know what you might find. Could be millions of dollars in there."

"You better sign that paperwork fast before this becomes public knowledge," Sue said to Ellen.

"I'll have to notify the owner of the property," Nancy said. "I'm sure she'll want to know what's in that safe before agreeing to anything."

"I thought you said the last owner died almost twenty years ago," Ellen said.

"His heir is the owner," Nancy said. "Charlotte Brewster. She lives in Colorado."

Ellen's stomach did a flip flop. Was there a chance the heir would increase her price or decide not to sell at all? "Will you keep me posted?"

"Of course," Nancy said.

Later, after Ellen and her friends had finished their breakfast at La Fonda and were waiting for the bill, Ellen called Rosario Cemetery to ask how she might go about getting someone to look for unmarked remains in the Rose Garden section. She was told she'd need proof of their existence—more than an article suggesting that the bodies might be there.

Ellen ended the call and said to her friends, "We need to call Bob Brooks. Remember him? The anthropologist at OU?"

"How could we forget?" Sue said. "He's the one who knew we had oil in Tulsa."

"Do you really think he'd come here to Santa Fe to help us?" Tanya asked.

"I think he'd love the opportunity to find and identify remains from the World War II era," Ellen said. "Don't you?"

"Absolutely," Sue said. "It would be another article for his academic belt—maybe even a book."

"Let's call him." Ellen looked him up in her contacts and gave him a call. She was surprised when he answered. She'd been expecting to leave a message.

"Hi, Bob, it's Ellen McManius—er, Ellen Mohr. Long time no see."

"Well, hello, Ellen. How are you?"

She caught him up to speed on their latest investigation and expressed her hope that he could bring his ground penetrating radar equipment to Santa Fe.

"Classes start in three weeks, so if you want me out there, it'll have to be quick," he said.

"I was hoping you'd say that," Ellen said with a smile. "How soon can you be here?"

That night, Ellen was visited in her dream by the old Japanese woman again.

"Please tell me you found him," the woman said.

"Who?" Ellen asked.

"My husband. Is he here? I thought he was here?"

"Mrs. Okada?" Ellen asked. "Is that your name?"

Ellen awoke before the old woman could answer. Ellen tried to revisit the dream but tossed and turned until morning.

Wednesday afternoon, Ellen and her friends met Bob Brooks at the Santa Fe airport in the rental. Ellen was surprised by how small the airport was—no bigger than a house.

"Howdy, ladies," Bob said as he entered the building from the tarmac, pulling a rolling case behind him.

"Hi, Bob," they said.

Ellen recalled the first time they'd met in his office at Oklahoma University. He hadn't been at all what she'd expected. He was tall and thin—except for a round pot belly—and had a receding hairline of white tufts and a short white beard. His blue eyes were stunning, but it was his smile that was the most unexpected aspect of him. Ellen had expected a pompous academic only to find a friendly, outgoing, and very relaxed earth digger.

"It's good to see you," Ellen added.

"Where's your machine?" Sue wanted to know.

"There it is." Bob flicked his thumb at a young man who walked in behind pushing a machine the size of a lawn mower. "I'll take it from here," Bob said to the young man. "Thanks."

Ellen took the rolling suitcase from Bob and led him toward the rental.

"They got any good food in this city?" he asked.

"You've never been to Santa Fe?" Sue asked.

"First time."

"I hope you like spicy food," Tanya said.

"Love it."

They loaded the machine in the back of the rental. Ellen was relieved it had fit. Then they drove to Rosario Cemetery to show Bob the rectangular plot known as Rose Garden.

"What a misnomer," he said of the name. "If this is a rose garden, I'm a monkey's uncle."

"Well, the truth in the second part of that sentence may not be contingent on the first," Sue teased.

"I'd forgotten what a character you are, Sue," he said.

"What can I say?" she said with a smile. "I try to do my part to make the world a better place."

"Speaking of making the world better," Ellen began, "how soon will you know if there are more bodies here?"

"Depends on how fast the cemetery will give me permission to investigate this area."

"Is there any chance they could say no?" Sue asked.

"There's always a chance, but I doubt they will, since there's enough circumstantial evidence."

From the cemetery, Ellen drove them to a Mexican restaurant, where Ellen and Tanya got salads and soup and watched in amazement as Sue and Bob ate the spicy enchiladas. Then they returned to La Fonda, where Bob checked in and everyone returned to their rooms to rest.

Since Ellen hadn't received an update about the house, she sent Nancy a text asking for one.

Nancy replied: *We have a professional scheduled to come to the property tomorrow morning to open the safe. I'll text you once I have an answer about the status of the property from the homeowner.*

What time tomorrow? Ellen texted.

Nancy replied: *Ten o'clock.*

Ellen kicked off her shoes and lay down on her bed with her phone to revisit the article about the Okada family's search for Haruto's remains. Finding a link to Ruth Okada's blog at the bottom of the article, she clicked on it only to discover that Ruth Okada was Haruto's granddaughter, and she'd spent her adult life searching for him. Ruth wrote: "Now that my grandmother, Toshiko, has passed, I want nothing more than to move my grandfather to his final resting place beside her, where he belongs. My parents—his son and daughter-in-law, Riku and Joy—are also buried there."

Scouring the blog posts, Ellen learned that Haruto was born in Seattle, Washington in 1920 and worked as a mechanic after high school until his girlfriend became pregnant. He promptly married and enlisted in the U.S. army in 1940 where he served for nearly two years. After the bombing of Pearl Harbor, he was reclassified as 4-C, or enemy alien, and imprisoned at the Tule Lake internment camp in northern California. The post said that Haruto wore his dog tags around his neck to remind the guards of his service.

"He was so young," Ellen said beneath her breath.

At the time of his death, Haruto must have been twenty-five. Ellen's son Lane would be twenty-five in a few months. She couldn't imagine him serving in a war, becoming a prisoner, being denied his constitutional rights, and fighting for control of his life until his death.

One of the blog posts described the conditions at the Tule Lake camp, claiming that it was an overcrowded high-security prison with trigger-happy guards and emotionally embroiled young Japanese American protestors. The center was built for fifteen thousand but was filled with over eighteen thousand men. They suffered poor sanitation, disgusting food, squalid housing, inadequate medical care, and unsafe working conditions.

Another blog post discussed what happened when Haruto and twenty-six other inmates refused to show up for their physicals after receiving their draft notices. They were put on trial, but, according to the post, the judge dismissed the case, saying, "It is shocking to the conscience that an American citizen be confined on the ground of disloyalty and then, while so under duress and restraint, be compelled to serve in the armed forces, or be prosecuted for not yielding to such compulsion." The draft resisters were released and returned to captivity in Tule Lake. In her post, Ruth asks, "Why would my grandfather, who had enlisted only to be reclassified as an enemy alien and who had been stripped of his citizenship and his constitutional rights, be willing to serve again?"

Ellen could only imagine how frustrated and angry Haruto must have been when he arrived, with over three hundred others from Tule Lake, at the Santa Fe camp in February of 1945. Although he was wrong to make death threats and use violence against the other inmates, he must have been nonplussed by their apathy toward the U.S. guards and other officials. According to Ben Nishimura, some of the guards in Santa Fe had even been friendly with his ancestors. The "troublemakers" from Tule Lake must have felt like they'd come to a strange land compared to what they'd experienced in their California prison. They had come to the camp ready to stir up loyalty for Japan after having been horribly betrayed by the United States, and they found nothing but incomprehensible resistance by their fellow Japanese American prisoners.

Ellen continued to scroll through Ruth Okada's posts until she stumbled upon one that was more personal than the others. In the post, Ruth wrote how difficult it was growing up with a grandmother who was obsessed with finding her husband. For years, Toshiko Okada believed her husband to be alive. Ruth wrote that her grandmother had a breakdown when Ruth was ten years old during which she finally came to terms with Haruto's death. But the agony didn't end there. Ruth wrote that, until her death, Toshiko refused to stop searching. She was desperate to find the man she loved and agonized over him being lost forever.

Ruth's mother and father died in a car crash when Ruth was five years old. From then on it was Ruth and her grandmother. Afraid that she would be tortured like her grandmother by a lost love, Ruth had never allowed herself to become close to anyone. There was only one man she'd spent her life looking for—her grandfather. Ruth wrote that when she turned sixty, she realized she'd wasted her life chasing a ghost.

Ellen wept for Ruth Okada. She wept for Toshiko, too. And although she was terrified of Haruto, she wept for him. None of them deserved what had happened to them.

Not wanting to give Ruth Okada false hopes, Ellen resisted sending her an email. As much as she wanted to let Ruth know about the efforts she and her friends were making to find Haruto's remains, she worried that things could still go very, very wrong—especially if Haruto were indeed the Shinigami that had caused over fifty deaths at Suicide Bridge.

Thursday morning, Ellen, Sue, Tanya, and Bob took the rental to the house on Luna Circle after breakfast, anxious to discover what was inside the safe in the secret bunker beneath the house. Bob had already talked to the staff at the cemetery and had put in a request with the city council for permission to use his ground penetrating radar machine on the Rose Garden lot. He'd received a call from a city official with approval but was cautioned not to dig. Ellen would drive him to the cemetery from the house on Luna Circle once the safe had been opened.

Nancy greeted them as they entered the garage and said, "He's just getting started and said it might be a while."

"I'd really like to be there when he opens it," Ellen said. "Mind if we wait down there? I remember there being a table and chairs."

"Suit yourself," Nancy said. "It's probably cooler down there than it is up here. I think I'll join you."

The group descended the stone steps and found the safe cracker sitting on the concrete floor in coveralls using a stethoscope to listen to the clicks as he turned the combination lock.

"Please be as quiet as possible," he said to them as they entered.

They sat in silence around the old wooden table. The chairs were full of dust and cobwebs. Ellen was wearing white capri pants that would probably need to be changed before lunch.

In less than half an hour, the safe was opened.

Ellen and her friends jumped to their feet and stood behind the safe cracker to peer inside the old metal box.

Nancy moved to the front of the group. She put on a pair of plastic gloves and, one by one, brought out the contents.

They included an old watch, a dusty book, some papers about the atomic bomb, and a role of cash. Nancy unrolled the cash and counted five hundred dollars.

"What's the book—just out of curiosity?" Sue asked.

With her gloved hand, Nancy opened it. "It says *My Life, by Chuck Jensen*. He was the original owner."

"How interesting," Bob said.

"Did you say Chuck Jensen?" Ellen asked, glancing at her friends.

"Yes." Nancy carefully leafed through the yellowed pages. "This appears to be his memoir."

"I would love to see it," Ellen said.

"Let me call Charlotte with an update," Nancy said. "I'll get back with you ladies as soon as possible."

Ellen realized that was their cue to leave. Worried that she might not ever see the memoir of Chuck Jensen again, she unlocked the sliding glass door to the back patio on their way to the front door. Sue noticed and lifted her brows but said nothing until they were in the rental.

"Are you planning on breaking in later, Ellen?" Sue asked once Ellen was behind the wheel.

"If I have to, yes," she said.

THE SHADE OF SANTA FE | 103

CHAPTER FOURTEEN

Chuck Jensen

By eleven o'clock Thursday morning, Bob Brooks was pushing his machine over the Rose Garden section of Rosario Cemetery while Ellen, Tanya, and Sue sat in the shade in the air conditioning of the rental, waiting. They hadn't been waiting long when Bob waved his arms at them, beckoning them to join him.

Ellen killed the engine and followed Sue and Tanya across the plot to Bob and his machine.

"Look at the radargram on the monitor," Bob said excitedly. "You see these hyperbolic reflections?"

"Hyperbolic as in exaggerated?" Ellen asked.

"As in an inverted parabola, or an inverted u," he said, pointing.

Ellen followed his finger to the inverted u shapes on the screen. "Yeah, so?"

"These are usually associated with burial mounds. I'm picking them up all over this plot."

"You mean in the areas where there aren't any marked graves?" Sue asked.

"Oh, yeah. In nearly every square foot of this plot."

Ellen glanced at her friends with wide eyes. "Does this mean...?"

Bob nodded. "The theory about unmarked graves is likely correct."

"But how can we prove it?" Sue asked.

"The next step is to dig. I'll need a permit from the city council. I'll apply for one online as soon as we get back to La Fonda."

Ellen gave Bob a hug. "Thank you so much."

"This helps me, too, so don't thank me. I'll get a solid paper out of this. After Tulsa, I got offers from Cambridge and Harvard. Did you know that?"

"No, I didn't," Ellen said.

"The wife and I didn't want to uproot our lives. Our kids were already settled in Norman and Oklahoma City."

"I totally get that."

Ellen walked alongside Bob as he pushed his machine toward the rental. Sue and Tanya led the way.

"All this excitement has made me hungry," Sue said. "Where should we go for lunch?"

When dusk arrived and Ellen still hadn't heard back from her realtor, she texted Sue and Tanya, asking them to meet her in the hall outside of their hotel rooms.

"What's up?" Tanya asked as she poked her head through her door.

Sue came out of her room a few yards away and walked over. Ellen waited for her to reach Tanya's door and then said, "I want to go back to the house."

"To break in, you mean," Sue clarified.

"We may never get another chance to see that book again," she argued.

"If it's even there," Tanya said. "Nancy may have taken it with her."

"It wouldn't hurt to check, would it?" Ellen asked.

"It would if we got caught trespassing," Sue pointed out. "But I'm always up for an adventure. I'll go with you."

Ellen and Sue turned expectantly to Tanya.

Tanya rolled her eyes and said, "Fine. I'll go, too."

Night had not yet fallen at eight o'clock when Ellen drove her friends in the rental along Luna Circle. She parked near the curb a few houses down so as not to draw suspicion by neighbors who might otherwise wonder what a car was doing parked at a vacant house. Then she and her friends quickly walked down the street and to the back of the property and let themselves into the home through the sliding glass door that led from the patio.

"Let's make this quick," Tanya said as she led the way to the garage, where the trapdoor to the cellar was still open.

Ellen followed Tanya down the stone steps using the flashlight on her phone to guide her. Then she turned on the generator and illuminated the room.

"It's here," Sue said. "We should take photos of it and get out of here."

Ellen crossed the room to the safe. "Good idea. Lay it on the table and I'll use my phone."

Sue and Tanya held the pages of the book open while Ellen snapped photos. But when she checked the quality of some of the images, she realized the writing was hard to read in the photos.

"It's easier to read the writing from the book than the photos. Why don't we read as much of it as we can tonight?" Ellen suggested. "When we're too tired to go on, I'll photograph the rest of the book, and we'll leave."

Sue shrugged. "I doubt Nancy would have any reason to come back by here tonight. The cash isn't in the safe, so she won't be worried about it being stolen."

"Fine," Tanya said. "But read quickly."

They sat around the table in the dusty chairs where Ellen began to read from the first page:

I was born on February 5, 1919, to Edith Cantu and Ray Jensen in Santa Fe at our place of residence near the railyard, which is now a commercial property.

Ellen looked up. "I'm going to skim through until I can find the relevant parts."

"Good idea," Tanya said.

Ellen skimmed through the next several pages and then found mention of 1940. "Okay, here we go."

In May of 1940, I took a clerical position at the post office. I had no idea at the time how dramatically this decision would change my life. A few years after I began working there, I was trained as a Post Office Inspector and was tasked with censoring the mail that came in and out of both the Japanese American segregation facility and the secret compound in Los Alamos known as the Manhattan Project.

Ellen glanced at her friends. "This is interesting. Should I keep going?"

"May as well," Sue said. "We don't even know what we're looking for."

"Look for mention of the bridge," Tanya said.

Both the prisoners at the segregation facility and the scientists and laborers at Los Alamos were instructed to write in English only, until we could hire translators, and to avoid certain subjects—a list of twenty-two to be exact. For example, the prisoners weren't allowed to complain about the conditions of their facility, including the food; nor could they criticize the government or spread propaganda. They were also prohibited from using the names of other prisoners or workers.

The scientists and laborers at Los Alamos had a similar protocol to their letter writing. Must be English, must not refer to other persons, must not include details about their work or about the compound, must not criticize the government or any of its agencies, etc.

The other censors and I had to comb through every letter, document, card, and postcard for the objectionable items and then either blot them out with black marker or cut them out using a sharp blade. Some letters looked like snowflakes by the time we were finished with them. Some had too many violations and had to be returned to the sender.

Some writers tried to bypass our methods by using invisible ink, which they made from milk, or juice, or urine. We also found messages on the back of the stamps. We censors were required to report such violations to our superiors, who would then take action against the offenders.

"This is interesting, but I'm going to skip ahead," Ellen said. "Let's see, he's talking about one of the scientists at Los Alamos. And now he writes about his friendship with the guards at the segregation facility. It's interesting that he calls it a segregation facility instead of an internment camp."

"Does he mention Jay West?" Tanya asked.

Ellen skimmed through the page looking for mention of Jay West or Haruto Okada.

"Jay West," Ellen said. "Listen to this."

In the spring of 1945, I got together with a couple of buddies, Jay West and Chayton Little, to celebrate the homecoming of our friend Rudy Castillo, who'd been a POW in Japan after being captured in the Philippines in Bataan. Jay was working as a guard at the segregation facility, and Chayton was home on leave while serving in the marines. After he'd had a few too many, Jay told us an interesting story. One of his detainees said that he'd swallowed a valuable sapphire before his relocation and, after excreting it, buried it somewhere on the prison grounds. Jay said the old man promised to give him the sapphire one day if he treated him and his fellow detainees with respect.

Narrowing her eyes, Ellen glanced at her friends. "Do you think the inmate was making that up?"

"What does Chuck say about it?" Sue asked.

Ellen skimmed through the pages. "Here it is."

I bought this house at 1124 Luna Circle while the neighborhood was still being developed, and I spent many days in search of the sapphire but as luck would have it never found it.

"Does he talk about the bridge?" Tanya asked again.

Ellen scanned for the words *bridge* and *ravine* but stumbled upon the name Haruto Okada instead. "Listen to this."

In mid-March of '45, Jay got Rudy and Chayton and me together again, but this time it wasn't for beer. It was to bury a body. Jay said the body belonged to Haruto

Okada, a Japanese American intern recently brought in with the Tule Lake bunch. Jay said the man had been inadvertently killed during a riot but hadn't been discovered until the following day. Rather than admit that he'd gone an entire day without noticing that one of his prisoners had gone missing, Jay recruited me, Chayton, and Rudy, along with one of the prisoners, to bury the body in secret in the pauper's field a half mile from the camp. A couple of groundskeepers asked what the hell we were doing. Jay paid them to keep their mouths shut. When Chayton tried to talk Jay out of the whole business, Jay said that the man who had accidentally killed the Jap was the same fella who'd buried the sapphire.

"We now have proof that Haruto's remains are buried here," Sue said. "We just don't know if the pauper's field referred to in that book is Rose Garden."

"Hopefully, Bob can answer that question," Tanya said. "I wonder if Ben knows anything about the sapphire."

Ellen massaged her forehead, where a headache had formed. "Do you think it's possible that the two groundskeepers Jay paid off might be the ancestors of some of the victims of Suicide Bridge?"

"Oh, that would make sense," Sue said excitedly.

"We should ask for the cemetery employee records from 1945," Tanya said.

Their conversation was interrupted by a rumbling noise overhead.

"Was that the garage door?" Sue said with a look of shock.

Ellen jumped up and cried, "I think it was. Hurry, grab a blanket and hide."

She reached up for the blankets stacked on the top of the shelving unit and tossed one to each of her friends.

"Turn off the generator!" Sue said in a loud whisper.

Ellen grabbed a blanket for herself and switched off the generator before finding her way to one of the cots along the back of the wall. She heard a car pull in overhead. Then the engine cut. Someone opened the car door, climbed out, and closed it. The garage door rumbled again as it closed.

Hiding beneath the rough army blanket on the dusty cot, Ellen prayed that whoever had arrived would not come down into the cellar, but her prayers went unanswered, and footsteps approached, descending the stairs.

"So, it's true," a woman said. "I can't believe we lived here for twenty years and didn't know this was here."

Ellen held her breath as the woman who must have been Charlotte Brewster inspected the cellar by the light of her cell phone. She prayed the woman wouldn't find the generator and turn it on. If she did, Ellen and her friends would have some explaining to do.

Suddenly, a scene from *I Love Lucy* popped into Ellen's head and made her want to burst into a fit of laughter. Realizing that the stress of the situation was making her delirious, Ellen covered her mouth and fought the giggles as tears streamed from the corners of her eyes.

A moment later, she heard the woman say, "Nancy, this is Charlotte. I just got in. Tell me you have the cash…oh, good. That's what I thought. And the diary?"

Ellen sucked in her lips as she recalled that they'd left the book on the table.

"No, it isn't here…oh, wait. I see it. Never mind. Yeah, I'll let you know. At least ten thousand, I would think. A third bathroom and a bonus room should be worth at least that. No, these pamphlets about the atomic bomb mean nothing to me. Neither does the diary or memoir or whatever—unless you think they're worth something?"

Ellen listened as Charlotte dropped the book back on the table and said, "Okay. Goodnight."

For a moment longer, Ellen held her breath and prayed. Then she heard the woman ascend the steps, get something out of the car, and open and close the door between the garage and the house.

Releasing the breath she'd been holding, Ellen sat up and pushed off the old army blanket. "You guys okay?"

"I nearly had a heart attack," Sue said. "Let's get out of here."

"How?" Tanya said. "We're stuck here until she leaves."

"And if she doesn't?" Sue said.

"You don't think she's planning to stay the night, do you?" Tanya asked.

"Maybe she brought an air mattress along," Sue said. "How long should we wait before we decide what to do?"

"I don't think we have a choice," Tanya said.

Ellen used the light on her phone to find her way back to the table. "I'm going to photograph more of these pages using a flash."

"I don't think I can sleep on this flimsy cot," Sue said. "There must be a way out of here. Tanya, why don't you sneak up there and see if the garage has a side door we missed."

"Why me? You're the one who doesn't want to stay."

"Because you're the stealthiest and least likely to get caught," Sue said.

Ellen continued to photograph as her friends argued over what to do.

"Fine," Tanya said.

Ellen was surprised that Tanya had agreed to go upstairs. She listened as Tanya ascended the steps and searched the garage.

Less than a minute had passed when Tanya returned. "There's no side door. What do we do?"

"Okay," Ellen said, thinking. "What's the worst thing that can happen to us if we get caught?"

"We get fined for trespassing," Sue said.

"You lose the house," Tanya said.

Ellen sighed. She wouldn't mind paying a fine or even spending a night in jail, but she didn't want to lose the house.

"I hear something!" Tanya said in a loud whisper. "Hide!"

The rumble of the garage door opening made Ellen's heart race. She crossed the room to hide on the cot beneath the army blanket and held her breath again as she listened to Charlotte get into her car and drive away.

"Hallelujah," Ellen said once the garage door had closed. "She's getting a hotel room."

"Or something to eat," Sue said. "We don't know whether she's coming back or not. Let's get out of here."

Back at the La Fonda, Ellen went to the business center to print the images she'd taken of some of the more interesting and relevant pages from Chuck Jensen's memoir. Then she met Sue and Tanya upstairs in Sue's room to go over them together.

"These photos are hard to read, even printed out," Ellen said once she was seated in a club chair across from her friends. "And Chuck's handwriting becomes more erratic toward the end. On the last few pages, he talks about his regrets. He says, 'I should have spent more time with Dorothy and the kids while I had a chance. I should have been a better father to Stephen. Maybe he'd still be alive.' I wonder if Stephen died at Suicide Bridge."

"Maybe Teresa Castillo knows," Tanya suggested.

"The last page doesn't even look like it was written by the same person," Ellen said. "And maybe it wasn't. It says, 'Chuck is gone. He's mine and won't be coming back.'"

Sue's eye widened. "That sounds like the Shinigami."

"Do you think Chuck killed himself on Suicide Bridge?" Tanya asked.

Ellen nodded. "Sounds like it. We should ask Teresa to confirm it."

CHAPTER FIFTEEN

Another Victim

Friday morning Ellen and her friends met Bob downstairs in the La Fonda restaurant for breakfast.

Once they were seated, the waitress came and took their order. By now, she asked Ellen, Sue, and Tanya if they wanted their usual, since they'd been eating there for nearly a week and ordering their favorite things on the menu. Bob asked for a stack of pancakes, and then the waitress left the table.

Bob said, "I've been emailing back and forth with the mayor about Rose Garden and the unmarked remains."

"Oh?" Sue asked. "Any progress?"

"He's given me permission to dig, with a very strict protocol, but nothing unusual."

"That's wonderful news," Ellen said.

"When can you start?" Tanya asked.

"I'll fly home tonight and begin assembling a team. Hopefully we can get on the road with our equipment tomorrow and start digging on Monday."

"That's fast," Tanya said before taking a sip of coffee.

"With school starting in less than three weeks, we have no choice."

"Well, thank you," Ellen said. "I can't say that enough."

"I'm doing this for me, too, remember? That reminds me, the cemetery emailed me that list of employees you asked for from 1945 and

'46," Bob said as he reached into his trouser for a folded piece of paper. "I printed out a copy for you."

"Oh, good," Sue said. "Can I take a look?"

He unfolded the paper and handed it over.

Sue put on her readers and skimmed over the page. "James Guerra and Larry Thompson are listed here. You were right, Ellen. They must have been the groundskeepers that Jay West bribed to keep silent."

"It's not something I'm happy to be right about, but it does convince me that we're on the right track."

"Speaking of unhappy things," Bob began, "I guess you haven't heard the news."

"What news?" Ellen asked.

"Someone offed herself on that bridge again."

"What?" Sue's expression matched Ellen and Tanya's look of shock. "We were just there."

"A body was found early this morning by someone walking his dog," Bob said. "A woman was hanging from the bridge. The authorities think she'd been there for a couple of days."

"Do they know who it is?" Tanya asked, her face pale.

"If they do, they haven't released that information to the public," Bob said. "The article I read online said it was a young woman, probably in her twenties."

"We've got to do something," Ellen said, feeling sick. "We could have prevented this."

"Now, don't blame yourselves," Bob said in a reassuring tone. "This isn't your fault."

"Call Father Yamamoto and find out when he can help us," Sue said to Ellen. "The sooner the better."

Ellen's spirits were lifted later that afternoon when Nancy called with Charlotte Brewster's new offer: she wanted ten thousand dollars more. Ellen was pleased and accepted. She'd been resting in her room after lunch, but now she was too excited to lay around. She popped on her shoes and headed down the hall to Tanya's room and knocked.

"What's up?" Tanya asked.

"I got the house!"

"Yay! I'm so happy for you!" Tanya gave her a hug. "I can't wait to go shopping!"

"Me, too. It's been a while since we've renovated. You *are* going to help me, aren't you?"

"I'd be disappointed if you didn't ask me to."

"Doesn't being here make you want to go back to doing Ghost Healers on a regular basis?" Ellen asked.

"Ask me after we see how it all turns out."

Just then, Sue poked her head into the hall. "What's all the commotion about?"

"Ellen got the house!"

"Well, we knew you would," Sue said. "It's not a huge surprise."

"I'm just so thrilled," Ellen said. "And excited."

"Well, I'm going back to my nap," Sue said. "Call me when you have something to tell me that I don't already know."

That evening after dinner, Ellen drove Bob to the airport so he could return to Norman to assemble a team to begin digging next week. An hour later, Ellen gathered with Sue, Tanya, Father Yamamoto, and Jane Connor on the back patio of the house on Luna Circle, even though Ellen hadn't officially closed on it yet. They had erected a folding card table at its center where they had placed three candles, a bowl of grapes, two standing makeup mirrors, a bowl of holy water, and a role of duct tape. Ellen sat on one of the lawn chairs with her elbows resting on the card table. She held a compact mirror in her trembling hands and opened it with the mirror facing her.

Sue and Tanya sat in the other lawn chairs at the table with her. Father Yamamoto and Jane stood behind Ellen, coaching her.

"The mirrors create a vortex," Jane was saying of the two makeup mirrors that were facing one another on either side of the holy water. "You'll want to hold the compact in between the two makeup mirrors when you call to him."

Ellen adjusted the position of the compact. "Like this?"

"That's right," Jane said. "Good. Now, if he appears in either of the makeup mirrors, keep talking to him. Keep the compact in position the entire time. That's important. If you move it out of position, this won't work."

"I still don't understand how she's going to trap him," Sue said.

"And shouldn't you be doing it?" Tanya asked Jane.

Tanya's face was paler than Ellen had ever seen it.

"It needs to be Ellen," Father Yamamoto said. "The Shinigami has already attached himself to her once. He will be angry that he was forced to leave her and will welcome the opportunity to victimize her again."

Ellen felt a chill creep down her back.

"But don't worry, Ellen," Jane said. "He won't be able to resist appearing to you in the mirror, to taunt you."

"Shouldn't we be worried that he can hear us?" Sue wondered. "What if he overhears our plan?"

"It wouldn't change anything," Father Yamamoto said. "Shinigami are very arrogant. He'll enjoy the challenge of trying to avoid our trap."

"Just keep the compact in position," Jane said again, "and wait for his face to appear in it. Don't jump the gun. Timing is everything."

Ellen took a deep breath. "Okay. Once I see him in the mirror, I snap the compact closed."

"No, no, no," Jane said. "You have to submerge it into the holy water first."

Ellen nodded, unable to control the tremble in her hands. "That's right. I submerge the compact into the holy water, and then I snap it closed."

"And then we dry it and tape it closed with several layers of duct tape," Jane said.

"And then what?" Sue asked.

"Then we hope it holds," Jane said.

"What if it doesn't?" Tanya asked with wide eyes.

"We'll be back at square one," Father Yamamoto said. "And I'll use the holy water to rebaptize everyone quickly, to drive him away."

Ellen gnawed on her lower lip, which was also slightly trembling.

"And what if it does hold?" Sue asked. "What then?"

"Well, it won't hold forever," Jane said. "We'll have no way of knowing how much time we have. It could be days, weeks, even years. We just can't know how powerful he is."

"Hopefully we can hold him off until after Sunday night's crossover ceremony," Ellen said.

They had decided to wait to conduct the ceremony on Sunday rather than Saturday, to give more families time to arrange to be there. Many of them wanted to come, even those who didn't believe. Ben Nishimura was among them. Ellen supposed they saw it as a memorial as much as anything.

Ellen asked Sue, "Have you received any more RSVP's?"

"Just about everyone whose email addresses I got from Teresa Castillo has said they'll be there—even Lizzy Little, though she doesn't know the victims that were related to her. But I still haven't heard from Teresa."

"That's surprising, since she's so devoted to the topic," Ellen said.

"She didn't seem too keen on the paranormal," Tanya pointed out.

"No," Ellen agreed. "Well, should we get started before nightfall?"

"Yes," Jane said. "I'm ready whenever you are."

"Me, too," the priest said.

Tanya lit the three candles. Then she and Sue reached across the table to hold hands. They each put their free hand on Ellen's shoulders.

Ellen said, "Spirits of the other realm, we come in peace. We mean no harm. We are looking for Haruto Okada. Haruto Okada, if you can hear me, please come to the light of these candles. Seek the aroma of our food, our offering to you."

One of the candles went out.

"Keep talking," Jane whispered. "I feel something."

"Haruto Okada," Ellen said again. "I'm so sorry about the way you died. I'm sorry that you never got to see your son or your granddaughter. I'm sorry you were never able to see your wife again. I'm sorry that the United States betrayed you, especially after you risked your life to serve this country. None of that was fair."

Suddenly, the face of the shade of Santa Fe appeared in all three mirrors.

Ellen looked up at Jane. "What do I do?"

"Wait until he's only in the one," she whispered.

"You thought you could trick me," he said to Ellen. "I'm smarter than you."

Another one of the candles went out.

"I mean you no harm," Ellen said.

"Liar. You mean to trap me."

"Only until I can find your granddaughter, Ruth. I want to bring her to you. She's been looking for you for her whole life."

"Liar!"

He shouted so loudly that one of the makeup mirrors cracked, causing everyone around the table to flinch with surprise.

"I'm telling you the truth," Ellen insisted once she'd recovered. "I want to help you. We all do."

"Others who have said that have betrayed me. My life was one betrayal after another. My death will be different—has been different."

His face was still glaring at her from all three mirrors. Ellen wouldn't be able to trap him until he was solely in the compact. And yet, she had no time to lose, because she could feel him reaching out to her again, attempting to attach himself to her.

"We've helped others like you to find peace," Ellen said, though she'd never helped a Shinigami before. "You need to move on."

"What makes you think you know what I need?" the shade asked angrily.

Ellen could feel him taking ahold of her.

"Don't you want to be reunited with your wife, Toshiko?" she asked.

The red eyes of the Shinigami widened.

"And your son, Riku," she added. "They're waiting for you on the other side."

Fearing for her life, Ellen used one hand to press the makeup mirrors face down onto the table, while she used the other to submerge the compact into the bowl of holy water.

"What are you doing?" Jane cried in a voice of panic.

Ellen's hands trembled violently, splashing the holy water onto the table. "I had to do something."

The Shinigami's red eyes widened even more, and he made a gurgling sound. Ellen slammed the compact shut and handed it over to Jane, who dried it with a hand towel before Father Yamamoto began wrapping the duct tape around it.

"Did it work?" Sue asked as she nervously popped a grape into her mouth.

"I think so." Jane put the compact into a Ziplock bag and zipped it shut, to keep it airtight. With a permanent marker, Jane wrote, "Do not touch" on the outside of the bag.

Ellen suddenly realized she'd been panting, on the verge of hyperventilating.

"You did it," Jane said. "Put your hands over your head and take a deep breath."

Ellen did as she was told as she smiled with relief at her friends.

Sue and Tanya patted her on the back.

"Geez," Tanya said. "I nearly fainted. Good job."

"I'm glad he didn't get you," Sue said to Ellen.

"So am I," Ellen said.

As frightened as she was of keeping the compact with her, Ellen was more terrified of someone coming upon it and opening it. She tucked it into her purse, and when she returned to her hotel room, she put it on the table, where she could see it, in case it opened. Then she poured a circle of salt around it and said a prayer to keep it closed.

With holy water nearby, she turned on the television to distract her as she readied for bed. She was about to call Brian to give him an update when she heard a reporter on the news announce that the recent victim on Suicide Bridge was Teresa Castillo.

Covering her mouth, Ellen broke into tears. Five days ago, Teresa had served Ellen and her friends freshly squeezed lemonade on her apartment balcony. The young woman had spoken with enthusiasm about her efforts to document the victims of Suicide Bridge. How had she become one herself?

Ellen glared at the compact sitting in the bag on the table, hoping in that moment that the Shinigami was suffering.

CHAPTER SIXTEEN

Renovation Plans

On Saturday after breakfast, Ellen met Nancy at the title company to close on the house on Luna Circle. Feeling grateful that something was going right in her life, she picked up Sue and Tanya from La Fonda and took them to her fixer upper to come up with a renovation plan.

They were standing in the sunken living room, assessing what needed to be done, when Ellen said, "I think I should start by picking out the granite for the kitchen countertops, and then I can pull all the colors and finishes from it. What do you think?"

"I think we should go look at some granite," Tanya said.

Sue took out her phone. "I'll search for places nearby."

Ellen went to the kitchen and opened some of the cabinets, undecided over whether she should replace them with white cabinets or wood. She wondered what the Property Brothers would do.

"There's a granite place on Cerrillos Road not far from Jane Connor's lab," Sue said. "Should we head over there?"

Ellen fished for the rental key from her purse. "Let's go."

As Ellen drove down Cerrillos Road, Tanya said from the passenger's seat, "I still can't believe you slept with that thing in your room."

"What choice did I have?"

"Couldn't you bury it behind the fixer upper?" Sue suggested.

"And risk critters or rain wearing down the bag and the tape?" Ellen asked. "Plus, how would I know if he'd broken free without constantly digging it up to check?"

"What if you keep it in the bomb shelter?" Tanya said.

"I thought about that," Ellen admitted as she stopped at a red traffic light. "But I guess I'm more worried about him taking another victim without me noticing than I am about him attaching to me. I feel I'm better armed, better equipped than most. I can get help from Father Yamamoto."

"True," Tanya said. "But still."

"I admire your bravery," Sue said.

"Thanks," Ellen said as the light turned green. "Poor Teresa. I still can't believe she's gone."

"Do you think it's our fault?" Tanya asked. "Not because we didn't stop the Shinigami in time, but because we might have led him to her?"

Ellen hadn't thought of that. Her happy mood over renovating her fixer upper plunged into guilt and despair. "Maybe so."

"I don't think so," Sue said. "He found the other descendants without our help. At least we're trying to do something. There's no reason why we should blame ourselves for any of this."

As Ellen turned into the parking lot of the granite outlet, she held on to Sue's way of thinking. "You're right. Suicide Bridge has been plaguing this city for decades, and we're the first to have a lead on why. We should be proud of ourselves."

Once Ellen had parked and turned off the engine, Tanya turned to her. "I love shopping for granite. I can't wait to see what you decide to do with the place."

Ellen's mood lifted again, and she smiled at her friend. "Let's go check it out."

They entered a front office where a receptionist asked, "May I help you?"

"We'd like to look at some granite slabs," Ellen said.

"Do you have a contractor?"

"Not yet," Ellen said.

"You need a contractor before you can enter the warehouse. We don't sell directly to the public."

Disappointment washed over Ellen in a long sigh.

"Is there a contractor you'd recommend?" Sue asked. "We're from out of town. She's just bought a fixer upper in Casa Solano."

From behind, a man asked, "What do you ladies have in mind?"

Ellen turned to see a young man in his thirties with beautiful green eyes that sparkled against dark skin and dark hair. He was tall and well built.

"Are you a contractor?" Ellen asked.

"Here's my card. If you'd like, I can escort you through the warehouse," he said.

"That would be awesome," Ellen said, taking his card and reading it. "Thank you, Ricardo."

He offered Ellen his arm, elbow out, bicep bulging, so she took it. Sue gave her a smile and a wink behind Ricardo's back and then turned bright red when Ricardo offered her his other arm.

"What service," Sue said as she took hold of his bicep.

Tanya rolled her eyes and followed the trio into the warehouse where the gorgeous slabs of granite awaited.

After looking at dozens of slabs and falling in and out of love with at least a half dozen of them, Ellen felt overwhelmed.

"It's a lot to take in," Ricardo said. "Maybe I can help you to narrow it down. First, let's talk about style. Are you looking for something modern or traditional? Or maybe something else, like old world or eclectic?"

"The architecture is mid-century modern," Ellen said, "but I tend to prefer traditional."

"Do you want something light and airy? Or do you want something warm and cozy?" he asked.

"Light and airy," Ellen said.

"Definitely," Sue agreed. "This will be an artist's studio and retreat. Light and airy makes more sense."

"You don't want to go with a southwestern look to match your location?" Tanya asked.

"We can make a southwestern design look light and airy," Ricardo said.

"I don't think I want to focus on a southwestern style," Ellen said. "Maybe I can bring in subtle elements, but I don't want that to be the theme, per se."

"Do you prefer sharp contrasts, like black and white, medium contrasts, like blues and creams, or monotone designs, like creams and whites?" Ricardo asked.

"He's really good," Tanya said.

Ricardo smiled at her. "Thanks."

Tanya's blush made Ellen giggle. They were acting like a bunch of schoolgirls.

"I like all of those looks," Ellen admitted, "but for this particular house, I think I'd like creams and whites with a pop of color here and there—like maybe yellow or light blue."

"Then I think I know which granite you need," he said. "Follow me."

Ellen and her friends followed Ricardo down the aisles of granite, focusing a little more on him and the way he filled out his jeans than on the beautiful slabs surrounding them. Sue kept glancing with lifted brows and a cheesy smile at Ellen and Tanya, expressing how pleased she was to be working with him. It took every ounce of self-control for Ellen not to bust out in hysterical laughter.

Ricardo turned down another aisle and came to a stop in front of a slab. He rubbed his hand over it and said, "This is called Starry Night."

"Like Van Gogh's painting?" Ellen asked.

"Exactly. As you can see, it has streaks of white, cream, and blue running through it, making these beautiful swirls reminiscent of the painting."

"It's gorgeous," Tanya said.

"You don't think it's too dark for light and airy?" Sue asked.

"I'm assuming you want white cabinets?" he asked.

"What do you think I should do?" Ellen asked.

"I would do white cabinets for light and airy."

"I suppose so," Ellen said. "Yes. Definitely."

"Then you don't want a countertop that's also too white. You want a little bit of contrast, and these light blue swirls can be picked up with pops of light blue throughout the home. You could even bring in yellow, because there are subtle flecks of it in here, too."

Ellen could see his vision. "I love it. These creams even go to brown and copper in some places. Wouldn't copper finishes look gorgeous with it?"

"But would copper be light and airy?" Sue wondered.

"Oh, yes," Ricardo said. "We can go with a light copper palette. It would be beautiful on white cabinets—the knobs or pulls—and on pendants hanging over the slab."

"I'm so excited," Ellen said. "How soon can you start?"

"It just so happens that I'm finishing up with a client this weekend. How does Monday sound?"

"Fabulous," Ellen said, unable to believe her good luck.

"I'll need to measure everything and give you an estimate before ordering your granite, but I can request a sample for you to take with you to the paint store." He pointed to the striations in the slab. "I'd recommend matching this cream for your interior walls and this whiter color for trim and baseboards—maybe even the kitchen cabinets."

"I love that idea," Ellen said. "What would you do for flooring? Tile or wood?"

"Well, a lighter color tile would add to the light and airy—maybe a travertine in this same family of creams. However, a honey oak would pick up on the copper tones here and in the knobs and fixtures."

"That's a tough choice," Tanya said. "Either one would be beautiful."

"I vote for wood over tile," Sue said. "It's easier to walk on—easier on the joints."

"But if it's an artist retreat, she won't be walking on it every day," Ricardo pointed out.

"True." Ellen tried to imagine the design first with the wood and then with the travertine. "I just don't know."

"When in doubt, go with wood," Ricardo said. "I love working with wood, and it never goes out of style."

Ellen giggled, recalling what Sue had said about Brian working on his wood. Tanya and Sue knew exactly why she was laughing. She could see it in their eyes. They couldn't hold back their giggles either.

"I'll keep that in mind," she said, laughing again.

"Did I say something funny?" Ricardo asked.

"It's a joke from earlier," Sue explained. "Just ignore us."

"Shall we head back then?" Ricardo offered Ellen his arm.

She took his bicep and sucked in her lips, trying to stop from giggling. This time, he offered Tanya his other arm. Tanya took it, her face soon the color of a tomato. Ellen could sense Sue's unhappiness behind them as they headed back to the front office—though Ellen was sure that the view perked Sue up.

A few minutes later, Ellen had her granite sample in hand and was heading to a Home Depot they had passed on the way to the granite warehouse.

"I can't wait to begin choosing fabrics and upholstery and light fixtures," she said, filled with excitement. "This is so much fun."

"I can't wait to see how it all looks when you're finished," Tanya said from the passenger's seat.

"I want to choose the color palette for my room," Sue said from the back seat. "I've already found the comforter set I want online."

Ellen laughed. "Oh, Sue. Why not?"

"Well, if she gets a room, don't I?" Tanya said with her brows raised.

"Of course, you do," Ellen said with a laugh. "Design away."

Then Sue said, "And I volunteer to be there on demolition day."

Ellen wrinkled her nose at Sue in the rearview mirror. "You just want to watch Ricardo."

"Why else would I volunteer?"

The three friends laughed again as Ellen pulled into the parking lot of Home Depot.

Saturday evening, when Ellen returned to her hotel room, the first thing she did was check on the compact in the plastic bag. Although it was still inside the circle of protection, it appeared to have been moved a few inches right of center. The hair stood up on the back of her neck. Had someone from the cleaning crew done that? Or had it moved on its own?

After she dressed for bed, she crawled beneath the covers and called Brian to update him on the house. She found herself staring at the Shinigami trap the whole time, even though the point of the call was to take her mind off it.

"I guess this means you aren't coming home anytime soon," Brian said with a voice of disappointment.

"I'm not sure how long I'll be. I don't plan to stay through the renovation—just until we get some closure for all these poor souls."

She hadn't told him about the Shinigami because she knew he would worry about her. If he knew it was in the room with her on a table just a few feet from her bed, he'd call her insane. Maybe she was insane, she thought.

"You could always come for a visit," she said—though she hoped he wouldn't, because then she'd have no choice but to come clean about the shade of Santa Fe.

"I can't this week," he said. "I'm flying to Portland for business. Maybe the week after—if you aren't back yet."

"That sounds good," she said, relieved.

"Lane didn't want me to say anything, because he doesn't want to put any pressure on you, but he's been wanting to have us over for dinner."

Ellen sat up in the bed, surprised. "Why didn't he say anything about it to me?"

"Because he knows you, and he doesn't want to interfere with your ghost healing."

"I'll give him a call tomorrow."

"Don't say I said anything."

"I won't. Promise."

"I miss you."

"I miss you, too. I love you, sweetheart."

"That's good to know," he teased.

It relieved her to hear the humor in his voice.

"I love you, too," he said. "Good night."

CHAPTER SEVENTEEN

Crossing Over

O n Sunday afternoon, Ellen and her friends met with Father Yamamoto and Jane Connor in the lobby of the rectory next to the cathedral to discuss their plans for the crossover ceremony. Everyone was sitting except for Jane, whose sciatic nerve was acting up.

"Are you sure you don't want to sit?" Ellen asked Jane. "There's room on the couch here with me and Tanya."

"No, thanks," Jane said as she paced nearby. "Walking is the only thing that helps. Don't mind me."

Father Yamamoto turned to Ellen. "How many people are you expecting for the crossover?"

"Sue?" Ellen asked.

Sue checked her phone. "I've got it in my notes. Let's see. Around seventy."

Father Yamamoto's eyes widened. "That's wonderful news. I didn't expect such a turnout."

"Well, not everyone was pleased with my email," Sue said, "or there would have been more."

"Not everyone liked being told that their loved ones have been unable to rest in peace for all these years," Jane said.

"I knew there would be some who would be offended," Ellen said, "but this isn't about them. It's about the dead."

"Well, those who are coming are bringing their spouses and children." Sue tucked her phone back into her purse. "It's going to be a family affair."

"Is there enough parking at the dog park?" Ellen crossed one leg over the other. "I haven't gone to look at it yet. I've been meaning to go see the Japanese American memorial plaque."

"Prepare to be underwhelmed," Jane said. "It's not much."

"We were lucky to get it at all," Father Yamamoto said. "There are still plenty of people in this city who aren't happy about it, including some of my own parishioners."

"Seriously?" Tanya asked with her mouth hanging open. "I find that shocking."

"I'm dead serious," the priest said. "There's a reason why Father Martinez presides during the most popular mass times."

Ellen frowned. "I'm so sorry, Father. I had no idea."

"It's only a handful of families," he said, "but the sting still hurts."

"The memorial plaque is actually quite nice," Jane said, amending her earlier comment. "It was good of the city to create a landmark so what happened won't be forgotten."

"That's what's important," Father Yamamoto agreed.

"And we're okay on parking?" Ellen asked again.

"Oh, yes," he said. "It's a big park with plenty of parking."

"I've emailed everyone with instructions," Sue said. "I've told them that we'll provide candles for an evening vigil. You did say that your choir would lead us in song, isn't that right, Father?"

"Yes. Not everyone from the choir can make it, but there are six that have confirmed."

"Good," Ellen said. "So, Father, you'll begin with an opening prayer, then the choir will lead us in song."

"I was thinking the choir should go early and be singing as people arrive, to add a sense of solemnity to the occasion," he said.

"Good idea," Sue agreed. "We can pass out the candles as people get there and they can join in the singing until we're ready to begin."

Father Yamamoto sat forward in his chair, leaning his elbows on his knees. "I'll do my opening prayer. Then Ellen can explain the purpose of the ceremony, after which the choir will lead us all in singing 'On Eagle's Wings.'"

"Perfect," Ellen said.

"How do you want the actual crossing over to happen?" Tanya asked. "Will Jane be leading it?"

"I don't think that's a good idea," Jane said from where she continued to pace. "Not after what happened ten years ago during my first attempt. Those spirits may not trust me. In fact, I don't think I should be there at all. Besides, I may need to stay on a heating pad all day tomorrow."

"Are you sure?" Ellen asked.

Jane nodded. "You can handle this. I know it, especially after I saw what you did with the Shinigami."

"Okay, then," Ellen said. "I'll do it."

She supposed she wanted to do it. She wanted to be the one to help the lost souls to the other side.

"We'll help," Sue said. "We can hold hands and use our energy together."

"You should ask each person there to say the name of a loved one who died at the bridge," the priest suggested. "That way they can be part of the ceremony, too."

"I love that idea," Tanya said.

"Me, too," Sue said. "Good idea, Father."

"I think it will help the trapped souls, too," Ellen said. "They should feel a connection with family, shouldn't they?"

"Absolutely," Jane said. "Everyone is connected, and the bond between family members is even greater."

"Even if they never met in person?" Ellen asked.

"Yes," Jane said. "*Like energy* binds with *like energy*. They might not understand it, but they will feel it."

Ellen decided to take Jane's word for it.

"We can end the ceremony with a final hymn," the priest said, "and hope for the best."

"Sounds like a plan," Ellen said.

"All this work has built up my appetite," Sue said. "Anyone in the mood for pie?"

"I have a zoom meeting in thirty minutes," Jane said. "I'll have to pass."

"I preside over the four o'clock mass," Father Yamamoto said. "I need to prepare."

"Four o'clock mass?" Sue repeated. "Won't you be cutting it close?"

"That's something I've grown accustomed to since my ordination."

"Why don't we go check out the memorial plaque at the dog park?" Ellen said to Sue and Tanya. "I'll take us for pie on the way back."

"I like the way you think," Sue said with a grin.

A cool breeze made the hike up the hill from the parking lot of the Frank S. Ortiz Dog Park pleasant, despite the effort it required. Tanya led the way, and Sue and Ellen struggled to keep up.

"It's just a bit further," Tanya said. "Are y'all okay?"

"I haven't dropped dead *yet*," Sue said, huffing.

Tanya led them to a circular concrete pad about fifteen feet in diameter on which sat a stone bench beside a large boulder that was taller than Tanya. From this vantage point, one could see the whole town of Santa Fe and its surrounding mountains. The memorial plaque was affixed to the boulder and read:

DEPARTMENT OF JUSTICE

SANTA FE INTERNMENT CAMP

At this site, due east and below the hill, 4555 men of Japanese ancestry were incarcerated in a Department of Justice Internment Camp from March 1942 to April

1946. Most were excluded by law from becoming United States citizens and were removed primarily from the west coast and Hawaii.

During World War II, their loyalty to the United States was questioned. Many of the men held here without due process were long time resident religious leaders, businessmen, teachers, fishermen, farmers, and others. No person of Japanese ancestry in the U.S. was ever charged or convicted of espionage throughout the course of the war.

Many of the internees had relatives who served with distinction in the American Armed Forces in Europe and in the Pacific.

This marker is placed here as a reminder that history is a valuable teacher only if we do not forget our past.

Information about this plaque may be found at the Fray Angelico Chavez History Library and Photographic Archives of the Palace of the Governors Museum or the New Mexico State Library.

Dedicated on April 20, 2002.

"It's rather beautiful," Ellen said. "Don't you think? I'm not underwhelmed by it at all."

Tanya nodded. "It's in the perfect location. At first, I didn't think a dog park sounded like the right place for a memorial, but the view from here overlooking where the camp once stood . . .it really is perfect."

Sue sat down on the stone bench to catch her breath.

"Shall we go have our pie now?" Ellen asked her.

Sue gave her a look of exasperation. "You may need to call a crane to get me down from here first."

Ellen rolled her eyes. "Oh, Sue."

"If I would have known how hard of a climb this was going to be, I would have waited in the car," Sue said. "Maybe I'll just stay here until after the ceremony, so I don't have to do that again."

"Come on. It wasn't that bad," Tanya said with a laugh.

"Easy for you to say," Sue said.

Ellen sat on the bench beside Sue. "We can sit here and rest for a few minutes. We're not in a hurry."

Tanya remained standing and gazed down at the valley below. "It's hard to imagine that this beautiful place was once a prison."

"I should paint it," Ellen said, just as the thought occurred to her. "I could paint two views of the same landscape—one with the internment camp and another as it is now."

"I can't wait to see it," Tanya said.

"Will you come up here to do it?" Sue asked.

Ellen stood up and took out her phone. "Maybe. Or maybe I'll just snap a photo."

As Ellen took her pictures, she thought about all the ways the land below had been occupied over the decades—from the Pueblo Indians to the Conquistadors, to the U.S. Department of Justice's prison camp, to the gorgeous neighborhood of Casa Solano and the plaza beyond it. She hoped her paintings would capture the landscape properly.

"Okay, I'm ready," Sue said. "And I sure hope the pie is worth it."

While they sat and drank their coffee and ate their pie at a bakery down the street, Ellen called Ben Nishimura to warn him that part, but not all, of his story would have to be made public to help the trapped souls cross over.

"We won't mention who killed Okada," Ellen explained over the phone. "But we need to reveal who buried him. It will soon become public anyway, because Chuck Jensen's memoir has been discovered, and I believe the homeowner who inherited it is trying to get a book deal."

There was a long silence on the other end of the line.

"Mr. Nishimura?"

"I'm here," he said. "I don't believe in this 'souls trapped' business, but if the story is going public because of Jensen's book, then I guess there's nothing more to be said."

He abruptly ended the call.

As dusk swept across the rolling hills of the Frank S. Ortiz Dog Park, one vehicle after another pulled into the parking lot. Men, women, and children made their way somberly up the dirt trails and past the memorial marker toward the edge of the ravine, on the opposite side of the bridge to the house on Luna Circle, where Ellen, Sue, Tanya, Father Yamamoto, and his choir were waiting.

Father Yamamoto had set up a folding table draped with white linens. A brass censer burning sage, frankincense, and myrrh sat at the table's center, surrounded by three unlit pillar candles. Beside these was a holy water sprinkler with a brass handle.

Sue and Tanya passed out tapered candles stuck inside round plastic wax catchers to people as they arrived. They lit the candles for a few people and asked them to share their flames with the others. One by one, bright spots dotted the top of the hill beneath the darkening sky as the angelic voices of the choir lifted toward the heavens.

Once it appeared as though everyone was there, the choir ended their song and Father Yamamoto lifted his palms into the air.

"Welcome and thank you for coming to this most extraordinary ceremony. I'm Father Yamamoto and I am here today with the choir of the Cathedral Basilica of St. Francis of Assisi and three paranormal investigators from San Antonio: Ellen McManius, Tanya Sanchez, and Sue Graham. We welcome you to this troubling place, a place that has brought all of us heartache and grief, to remember those that we've lost and to welcome them to the other side. First, we want to pray for their peaceful repose, something our paranormal investigators suspect has been denied them these many years because of the way they died. I'll let Mrs. McManius explain that in a moment, but first, please bow your heads and ask for God's blessing and pray that his heavenly angels and saints will open their arms and welcome the souls of our beloved departed home. Father, we ask this of you in your son's name, Jesus Christ, Amen."

"Amen," many of the people replied quietly.

Father Yamamoto then picked up the chain to the brass censer and walked around the crowd, swinging it back and forth, to allow the smoke from the incense to wash over everybody gathered there. He also carried the holy water sprinkler so that he could shake the holy water onto the spectators after he washed them with the smoke from the incense. He did this to protect them from wayward spirits who might try to attach themselves to their loved ones rather than cross over to the other side.

As the priest made his rounds, Ellen stood behind the table and faced the crowd. "Thank you, Father Yamamoto. And thank you, invited guests and relatives of the victims of this bridge behind me. In our investigations, we discovered a commonality among those who died here. They were all descendants of seven men involved in the secret burial of a Japanese American intern in March of 1945. The intern, Haruto Okada, had been killed during the brief riot that took place here with the Tule Lake prisoners. The guard on duty, Jay West, didn't notice him until the next day, when a prisoner named Kiyoshi Nishimura revealed where his body had been hidden. Rather than admit that he'd lost track of one of his prisoners or make trouble for the prisoner who'd found him, Jay West solicited the help of three friends—Rudy Castillo, Chayton Little, and Chuck Jensen—and bribed the groundskeepers on duty at the cemetery—James Guerra and Larry Thompson—and buried Okada in an unmarked grave with the help of inmate Nishimura. We based our conclusions on interviews we conducted with some of you and on entries in Chuck Jensen's handwritten memoir, only recently discovered. We believe the ghost of Haruto Okada has been taking his revenge on the descendants of those men by possessing them and bringing them to this bridge."

Several people in the audience gasped at this information, even though a shorter version of this had been explained in Sue's invitational email to them.

"I know this is troubling information that only adds to your grief over your lost loved ones," Ellen said, "but I'm not telling you this for your sakes. It's for the souls of your beloved departed lost here beneath Suicide Bridge that I inform you of this connection between the victims. They have been trapped here since their deaths because they didn't know that they had died. Having been possessed by Okada, who became what's known as a Shinigami, they weren't conscious during their deaths. Maybe you can take solace knowing they didn't suffer. Anyway, they woke up separated from their bodies and confused about their circumstances. Tonight, I plan to tell them what has happened to them and show them how to find their way to the other side."

Father Yamamoto, who had finished bathing the crowd with the incense and holy water, joined Ellen behind the table. Sue and Tanya, who had been standing to the side, joined Ellen, too.

"Before we get started," Father Yamamoto said, "I invite each of you to say the names of those you lost on Suicide Bridge. It's okay if you speak over one another. We just need to say the names to appeal to the spirits trapped below the bridge. Feel free to say their names more than once."

At first, no one said anything. Ellen could hear the crickets chirping. She glanced nervously at the priest, who frowned.

But then someone said, "Chuck Jensen. Stephen Jensen. Kara Connelly. Matthew Jensen."

Once the first person had spoken, many more followed.

"Polly Guerra. Tony Castillo. Beverly Little."

Ellen and her friends waited for five full minutes as loved ones said and repeated the names of those who were victims at the bridge. Tears fell down the cheeks of more than a few gathered there.

When the crowd grew quiet again, Tanya lit the three pillar candles that were on the table. Then she, Ellen, and Sue held hands with Father Yamamoto.

The crowd grew quiet as Ellen said, "Spirits of the other realm, we mean you no harm. We come in peace. We are here to help. We've called you by name. If you heard your name, or if you didn't hear your name but you are stuck among those who did, please know that you are surrounded by friends and family who love you. We want to help you get to where you belong. You were tricked into dying before your time. You were tricked by a vengeful spirit. We are so sorry for your tragic deaths, but we want to help you find peace. You need to go home to your loved ones, who are waiting for you on the other side."

Ellen took a deep breath as she looked out over the crowd. "I call upon the loved ones of those lost souls that have been trapped in the ravine beneath Suicide Bridge. I call upon God's heavenly angels and saints. Please open the doors of heaven and welcome these souls home. Please show them the way."

The choir then began to sing "On Eagle's Wings," and those in the crowd who knew the song sang, too. Ellen wished that Jane had come to the ceremony, because she couldn't tell if it was working. As she sang along with the others, she glanced at her friends with lifted brows. They shrugged as they sang, too. They didn't know either. No one knew if it was working.

Then, suddenly, all the candles went out at once—not just those on the table, but those held by the attendees, too. The voices of the choir faltered and eventually stopped singing. A gust of wind hadn't been the cause of the flames going out, because, although there was a slight breeze, it had been blowing steadily all evening. The people in the crowd gasped and began to whisper among themselves. A nervous energy filled the air. Had the candles been extinguished by their loved ones as they returned home? Or had the Shinigami returned?

"The Shinigami is trapped," Ellen tried to reassure everyone. "We wanted to help your loved ones to crossover before turning our attention to helping Okada. Father Yamamoto has protected you with incense and holy water. You have nothing to fear."

"Then are they at peace?" someone asked from the crowd. It was Darren Cole, widower to Angie Cole.

"Yes," Father Yamamoto said, though how he could say so with any certainty, Ellen didn't know. "Your loved ones have been welcomed home by God's heavenly angels and saints. Let us sing one more song in praise of God for this mercy he's shown us. Please feel free to return to your vehicles whenever you wish. You may keep the candles. Take them with you."

Then the choir sang "Glory to God" as the crowd gradually dispersed—all save Ben Nishimura who approached them with tears in his eyes.

"I felt something," he said. "I felt my daughter saying goodbye. I didn't believe, but now I do. Thank you."

Tears spilled down Ellen's cheeks as she squeezed the artist's hand. "I'm so happy to hear it, Mr. Nishimura."

"Please call me Ben."

Father Yamamoto shook his hand. "It's a pleasure to meet you, Ben."

To Ellen, Ben said, "Can we meet tomorrow for lunch? I have something more to tell you."

"Absolutely," Ellen said. "Why don't we meet at the restaurant in the La Fonda around noon?"

"I'll be there," he said.

As Ben Nishimura walked away, Sue said, "I wonder what that was about."

"I guess we'll find out tomorrow," Tanya said.

Then Ellen turned to Father Yamamoto. "Do you really think we were successful?"

"I saw them go," he said. "Not with my eyes, but with my mind's eye. You didn't see them?"

"No," Ellen admitted. "But I'm so relieved that you did."

CHAPTER EIGHTEEN

Penance

Monday morning after breakfast, Ellen drove her friends in the rental to her fixer upper to meet with Ricardo and to experiment with a few cans of interior paint. As she turned into the drive, she was shocked by what she saw. Someone had spray-painted *Demon Lovers* across the white garage door.

As Ellen parked the car, Tanya said, "What is wrong with people? We just helped over fifty souls."

"Seriously. Who would do this?" Sue said from the back seat.

Ellen rubbed her fingers over her forehead, trying to think. "We must have said something at the crossover ceremony about Okada that didn't sit well with his victims' families."

"But who knows that you bought this property?" Tanya wondered.

"The realtor, the guy from the title company . . . I don't know who else," Ellen said.

"I can understand why they'd hate the Shinigami," Sue said. "They don't like the idea of his suffering coming to an end. He killed their loved ones. He's a serial killer."

"It's strange to judge someone for things they do after their death," Tanya pointed out. "But I get it."

"I feel like he's suffered enough already," Ellen said. "And how we're punished after death, well, that doesn't seem like it should be up to us, does it?"

"Maybe they don't realize that as long as the Shinigami roams the earth, their families remain at risk," Sue said. "It's in their own interests for Okada to cross to the other side."

"Maybe Father Yamamoto could work that into his next homily," Tanya said. "The victims' families aren't all Catholic, but at least that could get the word out."

"Good thinking," Ellen said, climbing from the car. "Meanwhile, I'm going to use one of these cans to cover this up."

"But that's interior paint," Sue said, climbing out, too.

"I'm having this door replaced anyway."

"You should call the police first," Tanya said as she stepped out of the rental. "Want me to?"

"I doubt it will do any good," Ellen said, "but go ahead."

"You don't think they'll be back?" Sue asked. "Whoever did this? Won't they just do it again?"

"I hope they do," Ellen said. "Because, next time, I'll be ready for them."

Later that afternoon, after they'd reported the vandalism to the police, accepted Ricardo's estimate, and painted over the offending words, Ellen and her friends returned to La Fonda to tidy up, and then they met Ben Nishimura for lunch downstairs.

"Thanks for meeting with me," he said once they were seated and had given their order to their waiter. "I can't thank you enough for what you did yesterday. It's the first feeling of peace I've had since losing my daughter."

"What was her name?" Sue asked.

"Jenna. She was only nineteen when she died."

"I'm so sorry," Ellen said. "I hope you'll take comfort in knowing that she's finally at peace."

"You made a believer out of me," he said. "I called my ex-wife last night. It was a good conversation."

"Any chance the two of you might . . .?" Sue lifted her brows expectantly.

Ben chuckled and shook his head. "She remarried years ago."

"But is she happily married?" Sue persisted.

"Sue!" Ellen scolded.

Ben laughed again. "Yes." Then he added, "Listen, in addition to thanking you for last night, I want to warn you about something that you might find once you start digging for Okada's remains."

"Sounds ominous," Ellen said before taking a sip of her water.

"I don't know if this story will have any bearing legally on what happens but hear me out."

"We're listening," Sue said.

Ben took a swallow of his tea and then said, "My great-grandfather, Kiyoshi Nishimura, came into possession of a pure blue star sapphire as large as an olive and uncut—which made it even more valuable. I was never told how he came to have it, only that he did. When he learned that he was going to be relocated without any guarantee that his shop would still be there on his return, he took the sapphire with him and swallowed it, so that his captors would not find it."

"So, it was true," Ellen said.

Ben lifted his brows in surprise. "You've heard this before?"

"Chuck Jensen wrote about it," she explained.

"Your great-grandfather told Jay West about it, who then shared the information with Chuck," Sue added. "Apparently, your great-grandfather promised to give it to Jay if he treated the prisoners with respect."

Ben nodded. "My father told me that, too. However, after my grandfather, Ren, killed Haruto Okada, my great-grandfather wanted the stone to be buried with Haruto as a form of penance. The night they buried him, Kiyoshi dropped the sapphire into the dirt with Haruto Okada's remains while the others weren't looking."

Ellen straightened her back. "Are you saying that there's a good chance that Dr. Brooks will discover the sapphire?"

"If Okada is buried there, then so is the sapphire," Ben said. "My lawyer is looking into the question of ownership for me right now. You see, I don't want you or the scientists or the university or the cemetery or the state of New Mexico to take possession of it. There will likely be a legal battle, I'm sure. I feel it is only right that the sapphire goes to the closest living relative of Haruto Okada, and my lawyer and I will fight to make that happen."

Tears sprang to Ellen's eyes, and she smiled warmly at the artist. "I'm so happy to hear that. His granddaughter, Ruth Okada, has been looking for his remains for as long as she can remember. The sapphire won't take away her pain, but maybe it will give her some comfort."

"It might offend her," Ben said. "She may feel my great-grandfather put a price on her father's life. I don't want her to think that I'm trying to buy her forgiveness."

"Maybe it's time for the two of you to meet," Ellen said just as the waiter brought their food. "What do you think? Should I arrange it?"

"I would like that," Ben said. "Thank you."

After lunch, Ben followed Ellen and her friends to Rosario Cemetery, where Bob and his team had erected a large canvas tent enclosing the area, as per the city's protocol.

"Wow," Tanya said as Ellen drove near the Rose Garden section. "People might think the circus came to town."

"It's massive," Sue said from the back seat.

Ellen parked on the side of the road. Ben pulled up behind her. Then she led Ben and her friends into the tent.

Eight people in addition to Bob were hard at work on the ground inside a four-foot-deep trench they'd already dug with an excavator across the entire plot. Piles of dirt added an earthy smell to the tent, along with the scent of sweat and body odor.

"Welcome," Bob said as they entered. "My students and I have been hard at work."

"I can see that" Sue said.

"Bob, this is Ben Nishimura, the artist we told you about," Ellen said to Bob. "Ben, this is Dr. Bob Brooks, the anthropologist in charge of the excavation."

"It's a pleasure to meet you," Bob said to Ben as he removed his dirty glove to shake hands.

"Likewise," Ben said.

"We're only just now reaching human remains," Bob explained. "We've recovered one body over here. Let me show you."

Ellen wasn't particularly excited about looking at skeletons, but she followed Bob hoping that the dead may have answers.

He led them to a long table where the recovered bones were laid out with the skull on the right and the foot bones on the left. Not every bone was in place, but there were enough parts to give the overall shape.

"Could this be Okada?" Sue asked.

"Not if he was twenty-five when he died. These are the bones of an old man," Bob explained. "We'll be able to determine more about him at the lab."

"What about over there?" Ben asked, pointing to a collection of bones on a second table.

"The beginnings of another body, also male, somewhat younger. It's possible those belonged to Okada. We'll need to run a DNA analysis against any living relatives of his to confirm."

"Can you tell how long they've been buried here?" Ellen asked.

"So far, the condition of the bones is consistent with your theory that they were buried in the 1940's." Bob said.

"Dr. Brooks!" a young man called from the other side of the dig. "Take a look at this!"

"Excuse me," Bob said as he left the table.

He hurried across the site. The young man used a fine brush to sweep the dirt from something he was holding in his hands. Ellen and the others followed.

"What is it?" Sue asked.

Wondering if it might be the sapphire, Ellen leaned forward.

"Dog tags," Bob said with a huge grin. "You won't believe what they say."

Ellen's knees felt weak, so she grabbed onto Tanya for balance.

"What?" Ben asked.

"Haruto Okada," Bob said.

Ellen went down on her knees and touched one of the dog tags. A strange sensation shot through her as tears fell down her cheeks. "You've found him. I can't believe you've found him."

A few hours later, Ellen and her friends returned to La Fonda to clean up before dinner. When Ellen entered her hotel room, the first thing she did was look for the Shinigami trap on the table. To her utter shock, it was gone.

The circle of salt was there, as was the Ziplock bag. The bag was opened, and the compact wasn't in sight. Ellen looked under the table and the beds and all around the room.

"Where is it?" she said aloud with both fear and frustration.

She called Sue to tell her what had happened.

"Report it to the hotel manager," Sue said. "Maybe someone from housecleaning took it."

"But why?" Ellen said.

"Who knows, but at least that's a place to start."

Ellen hung up with Sue and called the front desk to report it missing to the hotel manager. "This isn't an ordinary compact. It's very, very important that I get it back. Please make this a top priority. Let your employees know that there's a $200 reward for anyone who has information about its whereabouts."

After she hung up with the hotel manager, Ellen texted Father Yamamoto and Jane Connor, to warn them. Then she called Tanya.

"I didn't want you to think I was keeping you out of the loop," Ellen added after she'd told her friend what had happened.

"Oh, my God, Ellen, this is terrifying," Tanya said. "What if it's broken free from the trap and is coming after you? You shouldn't be alone. How do you feel?"

"Fine. I'm going to take a quick shower, and then I'll meet you at Sue's in about ten minutes."

In the shower, Ellen rinsed the dirt from the graveyard from her arms and feet. Then she dried off, put on fresh clothes, and added just a little makeup. As she did, she thought about the bones of Okada. She should be happy that she and her friends could put an end to Ruth's lifelong search, but only sadness filled her heart. Such wasted lives. That's all she could think about.

She slipped on her shoes, grabbed her purse and keycard, and headed over to Sue's.

Tanya met her in the hallway. "Any word from the hotel manager?"

"No," Ellen said as she tapped on Sue's door.

Sue opened the door, and they followed her inside.

As Ellen collapsed on one of the club chairs, she said, "I can email Ruth Okada through her blog. Want to help me write it?"

"Sure," Sue said. "Remind me next time to bring a laptop."

"I won't forget mine, that's for sure," Ellen said. "I hate using my phone to write long emails."

"I brought my iPad," Tanya said as she pulled the pad from her tote. "Why don't you dictate, and I'll type?"

"Okay," Ellen said. "Thanks, Tanya. Let's see. Can you go to her blog and find the contact page?"

"Doing that now," Tanya said.

"While she's doing that, let's figure out where we're going for dinner," Sue said. "I don't think I can eat downstairs again. How does steak sound?"

"Whatever you guys want is fine with me," Ellen said. "I'm not sure I can eat, to tell you the truth. I can't shake this feeling of sadness. I keep thinking about Teresa Castillo and all the other victims of Suicide Bridge. And poor Ruth Okada and her entire family. Haruto was so young when he died. It's all just overwhelming, isn't it?"

"Try to focus on the good we're doing," Tanya said.

"That's right," Sue said. "You should feel good about bringing peace to so many lost souls. I know I do."

"I guess I'm reminded of how many years they suffered," Ellen said as tears pricked her eyes. "Sometimes I wish we'd never come here."

"Don't say that," Tanya said. "How can you say that? If we hadn't come, those souls would still be suffering."

Tears spilled down Ellen's cheeks. "I know. You're right. But isn't the thought of everything that has taken place here overwhelming either of you? It's got me so down."

"I found Ruth Okada's email," Tanya said. "What should I write?"

"Start with *Dear Miss Okada*," Sue began.

"I've got that much," Tanya complained.

Sue said, "How about this:

"*My friends and I were investigating the internment camp in Santa Fe when we came across your blog. We're pleased to inform you that we believe we have found your grandfather's remains at the Rosario Cemetery, where a team of anthropologists are uncovering a series of unmarked graves. We also believe we have discovered the truth as to how your grandfather died. If you would like to meet with us, please reply to this email. Yours Truly,*

"And then add our names," Sue said.

"That sounds good," Tanya said. "Don't you agree, Ellen? Should I hit send? Or do you want to add anything?"

"Why don't you copy it to all of our email addresses," Sue suggested.

Ellen got up to get the box of Kleenex from Sue's bathroom.

"Ellen?" Tanya asked.

When she returned, Ellen said, "It sounds fine. I'm sorry. I feel so blue."

"Maybe dinner will cheer you up," Sue said. "I found a steakhouse on the northside of town that has great reviews."

CHAPTER NINETEEN

Demolition Day

E llen was painting the finishing touches on her Palo Duro Canyon landscape in her backyard studio when the door suddenly
opened, startling her. Fortunately, the brush hadn't been on the
canvas, or she might have messed it up.

"Mom?"

Ellen turned to see Lane standing in the doorway in his pajamas.

"What's wrong, honey?"

He sighed. "Aren't you going to tuck me in? It's past my bedtime."

"Is it? Already?" She glanced at the clock on the wall. "You're right.
I'll be right in. I just need a few more minutes."

"That's what you said twenty minutes ago," he complained.

"Well, honey, really," she began, feeling irritated. "You're in the sixth
grade. Do you really need your mother to tuck you in?"

Lane's mouth dropped open and his brows furrowed before he ran
back to the house.

"Oh, honey!" she called. "I didn't mean that!"

She dropped her brush into a cup of water, wiped the paint from her
hands, and followed Lane inside. She found him in his bed with his back
turned to her.

"I didn't mean that," she said again. "I love tucking you in."

"No, you're right. I don't want you to."

Ellen crouched down on her knees and combed his blond hair with her fingers. "Please?"

"Leave me alone, Mom. I want to go to sleep."

She decided not to press him. He was angry and needed to be left alone.

"Okay, sweet boy. I love you."

She waited for him to reply, but he didn't. He wanted to hurt her, too. She understood and could kick herself for losing her patience and saying words she could never take back. As she went down the hall to check on Nolan, tears sprang to her eyes. Lane would probably never let her tuck him in again.

When she reached Nolan's room, she found him awake beneath his covers.

"Time for lights out," she said just before she kissed his cheek.

"I'm mad at you," he said.

"What? You, too? Why?"

"Today was the last day to turn in my permission slip for the science fair. I've been asking you to sign it all week. Now I can't do it."

"I'll talk to your teacher in the morning, honey. I'm sure I can straighten it all out."

"She told us to tell our parents not to call her or email her about it. A deadline is a deadline."

Ellen noticed tears in Nolan's eyes.

"Oh, honey. I'm so sorry. But there's always next year."

He turned his back to her and said nothing in reply.

A lump rose in Ellen's throat as she turned off the lamp and left Nolan's room. She crossed the hall, where she found Alison asleep with her favorite picture book opened beside her. Alison had been waiting for Ellen to come read to her, and Ellen had lost track of time again.

Ellen closed the book and put it on the table beside the bed. Then she sank to her knees and wept. She'd let all three of her children down in the course of a day. She was a terrible mother.

Paul poked his head inside Alison's door. "Honey? Are you coming to bed?"

"Not yet," she said through her tears.

"Of course not," he muttered. "Well, good night, then."

Ellen lay on the floor in her daughter's room and wept some more. She was a disappointment to everyone in her family.

After some time, she woke up on her daughter's rug with swollen, wet eyes. She climbed to her feet and headed toward her room, closing Alison's door behind her.

"Ellen?"

"Hm?" Ellen turned, expecting to find Paul but found Sue instead.

"Ellen, are you okay?" Sue asked.

"What?" Ellen blinked and found herself in the hallway of the La Fonda. "Oh, I was having a bad dream. I must have been sleep walking."

"Are you locked out of your room?" Sue asked, trying the handle on the door. "I was just heading down to the vending room for a midnight snack. It's a good thing I found you. Why don't we go downstairs and ask for another key?"

"But I'm not dressed," Ellen said.

"I'll fetch you one of my robes," Sue said.

Ellen went with Sue for a robe, and then together they asked for an extra key at the front desk, but without an ID, the woman behind the desk couldn't issue them one.

"Her purse is locked inside her room, with everything else," Sue explained. "Can't you come with us, and she can show you her ID after you let her in?"

"I need to stay at the front desk," the young woman said, "but I can call security to help you."

"No, that's okay," Ellen said. Then she turned to Sue. "I'll just sleep with you tonight, if that's okay."

"You're going to need to be let in eventually, Ellen," Sue said. "Why not get it squared away tonight so you can sleep in your own bed?"

"Alright, then."

Sue nodded to the woman at the front desk, who then telephoned security. Within five minutes, a bald Hispanic man in his thirties appeared in a white uniform. The young woman behind the desk explained Ellen's predicament and handed him a key to her room. They took the elevator up, and he let her into her room. She fetched her ID and thanked him again.

"Good night, ladies," he said before he left.

"Good night," Sue said. Then to Ellen, she said, "I'm going to get some Ding Dongs down the hall. Want anything?"

"No, thanks. Good night, Sue."

"Good night. Don't forget to close your circle of protection."

"I won't forget."

After she secured the circle of salt, Ellen lay down in her hotel bed thinking about how she had hurt Lane the night she told him he didn't need her to tuck him in. Tears welled in her eyes as she wished she could go back in time and stop herself from saying those words. Her sweet little boy was only twelve or thirteen at the time. Soon, on his own, he would have stopped calling her to his room asking to be tucked in. If only she could have made it last as long as it could instead of losing her patience.

The next thing she knew, she was standing beside her mother, Ima, and holding on to her father's arm. Ima smiled as Jody, Ellen's brother, led her down the aisle of a church full of people. Then her father led Ellen down the aisle to where Paul was waiting.

Paul looked handsome in his gray tuxedo. His brother Gordon stood beside him. Just as Ellen was about to join Paul at his side, where the priest stood on the dais before the altar, someone called out to her.

She turned to see Brian coming toward her from the back of the church.

"Ellen? I thought you loved me?" Brian said with a face full of tears.

"Brian? Of course, I do," she said.

She turned to Paul, and her heart nearly broke in two.

"What's going on?" Paul asked her. "Who is this man, Ellen?"

"He's my, my . . .he's my husband," she said.

Ellen gasped and opened her eyes to find herself in her hotel room in La Fonda. Tears poured from her eyes as she pressed her face into her pillow and wept.

"I love you, Paul," she whispered. "I'm so sorry. I'll always love you."

Tuesday morning came early for Ellen when she was awakened by the ringing of the telephone—not her cell, but the hotel phone.

"Hello?" she asked as she glanced at the clock. It was seven a.m.

"Sorry to wake you, Mrs. McManius. This is Rueben Perez, the hotel manager. I thought you'd want to know as soon as possible."

"Know what?" she asked as she rubbed her eyes.

"One of my housekeeping staff has come forward about your missing compact. I have her here in my office if you'd like to come down and speak with her. It goes without saying that she will no longer be working here. This may be your only chance."

"I'll be right down."

Ellen jumped out of bed and quickly dressed and brushed her hair and teeth. Then she slipped on her shoes, grabbed her purse, and headed downstairs.

The hotel manager was waiting for her at the front desk. He took her back to his office, where a young woman was sitting on a chair, crying.

"Norma, this is Mrs. McManius," the manager said. "Please tell her what you told me."

The woman reminded Ellen of Alison—long dark hair framed a sweet round face. Her mascara was smeared around her eyes from crying.

"I'm so sorry, ma'am," Norma said. "I never intended to take it. I was just curious, that's all. I only wondered why it was taped up. I just meant to take a quick peek inside. I was careful not to break the tape. I just got it wet under the sink and slipped it off, planning to slip it right back on. But when I opened the compact, the mirror inside of it cracked for no reason. I swear. It startled me, and I dropped it, and the whole thing came apart."

"What did you do with it?" Ellen asked, trembling now that she knew for certain that the Shinigami was free.

"I threw it away. I'm so sorry, ma'am. I didn't know how important it was to you."

The hotel manager cleared his throat. "I've already asked the rest of the staff to search the garbage, by the off chance it's still on the premises."

"That isn't necessary," Ellen said. "You can call off the search. It's no good to me now."

"I can't say I'm sorry enough, ma'am," Norma said.

"It's okay," Ellen said, opening her purse. "Thank you for coming forward and for being honest about what happened." Ellen took out two one-hundred-dollar bills and handed them to the young woman, but Norma refused.

"I don't deserve it," she said with her face in her hands.

"You're going to need it now that you're without a job," Ellen said. "Take it."

Norma wiped her eyes and then wiped her hands on her pants before accepting the money. "Thank you, ma'am."

"You can go now, Norma," the hotel manager said. "You'll get your last check in the mail next week."

Norma rushed from the room.

"Please accept my sincere apologies, Mrs. McManius," Mr. Perez said. "I'd like to compensate you with two nights' on us, along with free breakfast for the duration of your stay."

"Thank you, Mr. Perez. I appreciate that."

As Ellen was returning to her room upstairs, she received a text from Tanya.

Call me after you've read Ruth's email.

Back in her room, Ellen sat on the bed and opened her email on her phone. She found Ruth's reply and opened it.

You have no idea how happy you have made me. I just booked the first flight out to Albuquerque this morning. There were no flights direct to Santa Fe. I should land today by 2:30 and be in Santa Fe before four o'clock and will go directly to the cemetery. Please ask Dr. Brooks to wait for me. I've been waiting for this moment for sixty years and can hardly believe it's really happening.

Yours Truly,

Ruth Okada

Tears sprang to Ellen's eyes. She should be happy, but she only felt sadness for the years of heartache Ruth and her grandmother had endured. She texted Ben Nishimura the news, suggesting that he meet them at the excavation tent at 3:30 that afternoon.

He immediately replied that he would be there.

Ellen phoned Tanya to update her about Ben's plans to meet them at the cemetery but decided not to mention what she'd learned about the compact. She couldn't bear to worry her friend. A voice inside her head reminded her that Tanya hated to be left out of the loop, but another voice silenced it.

"Have you been crying?" Tanya asked over the phone.

"I'm just so sad," Ellen said. "Their lives were needlessly ruined. It breaks my heart."

"Come on, girlfriend. It's demolition day, remember? We get to see Ricardo again."

Ellen laughed at her friend. "We're such schoolgirls, aren't we?"

"Nothing wrong with that! Let's get Sue out of bed and get this day going."

"One mention of Ricardo ought to do the trick."

After breakfast, Ellen drove her friends in the rental to meet Ricardo and his team at the house on Luna Circle. Two men were carrying parts of the kitchen cabinetry through the garage and dumping them into a large trailer that was parked in the driveway.

"Wow, they aren't wasting any time, are they?" Tanya said as Ellen pulled up to the curb.

Once inside, Ellen found that all the carpet had already been removed. Four men, including Ricardo, were destroying the kitchen.

"Hello, there," Sue called from the sunken living room.

"Take ten, guys," Ricardo said to the others. Then he removed his gloves and came to the living room, where he shook each of their hands. "How are you ladies doing today?"

"Not as fine as you," Sue whispered loud enough for everyone to hear.

Ricardo blushed and laughed.

"Oh, did I say that out loud?" Sue said, blushing, too.

"We've made a lot of progress, as you can see," Ricardo said, quickly changing the subject. "Excuse the dust. It's everywhere."

"Yes, it is," Ellen said, waving her hand in front of her face. "You're further along than I expected."

"Your new cabinets should be ready tomorrow, and the floors are arriving on Thursday."

"Sounds like everything's coming along nicely," Ellen said. "You might finish in less than six weeks, at this rate."

"I doubt it," he said. "A lot still has to happen. And you haven't told me what you want me to do with the basement. Have you decided anything?"

"For now, just clear everything out. I'll probably just use it for storage."

"Yes, ma'am. Will do. Have you had a chance to pick out a backsplash?"

"Not yet," Ellen said. "We'll go shopping for that tomorrow. I promise. I already have some ideas."

"I have a question about the master bath, too. Can you follow me?"

Ricardo led them through the master bedroom to the bath, where the tub, vanity, and toilet had already been removed. Ricardo was worried that the new vanity Ellen had originally chosen wouldn't fit with the new toilet. He pulled out his phone and showed her two other options that he thought would work better. Sue and Tanya helped her to make the decision.

Then he showed her a plumbing leak he found in the master bath between the faucet and the shower head. "I'll need to open up the wall to find the leak. It's likely that some of the plumbing may need to be replaced."

"That's fine," Ellen said. "One expects this kind of thing in houses this old."

"Okay, good," Ricardo said. "That's all for now. I'll keep you updated. The sooner we can order your backsplash, though, the better. Oh, one more thing."

"Yes?" Ellen asked.

"Someone painted those unkind words on the front of your garage door again."

"So, they *did* come back," Sue said.

"That was fast," Tanya said.

"The security cameras haven't been installed yet," Ellen said. "Would you mind painting over the words for me before you leave, Ricardo? Just add it to my tab."

"Sure. No problem," he said.

"The cameras are being installed this afternoon," Ellen said. "So be on the lookout for a company called Home Security."

"Will do," Ricardo said.

"Thanks," Ellen said. "I think I'll go outside for some fresh air."

"You okay, Ellen?" Sue asked as she followed Ellen and Tanya onto the back patio. "Your eyes are red."

"I think it's the dust," Ellen said. "That and all the crying I've been doing lately. I had horrible dreams last night. I can't seem to shake off the sadness."

"Think about how gorgeous this place is going to look when Ricardo is finished," Tanya said. "Maybe we could check out some tile today. We have time, don't we?"

"I need to get away from all this dust," Ellen said. "I'm going up the hill for some fresh air. I'll be right back."

Ellen ascended the steps to the back of the property and looked out onto the dog park across the ravine. Then she turned around and looked down on the house, on the neighborhood, and on the plaza beyond. She wondered how many people had looked out from this vantage point onto the internment camp during the years it had existed. What did they think as they gazed down on the prisoners? Did they feel safe? Ashamed? Both?

She wiped the tears from her eyes and turned back to the ravine, thinking about all those poor people whose lives had needlessly ended on Suicide Bridge.

"Ellen?" Tanya called from behind. "What are you doing?"

"I'm . . . ." Ellen blinked. She hadn't realized that she'd stepped onto the old bridge. "I don't know."

Her knees had begun to feel weak and shaky, so she held onto the railing to keep her balance.

"Let's go," Tanya said as she took Ellen's hand and pulled her from the bridge. "I think we should go and see Father Yamamoto."

"I'd rather go shopping for tile."

"You don't feel sick?" Tanya asked.

"I feel fine."

"Good. Let's go shopping, okay?"

Ellen's heart was beating fast as she nodded and said, "Okay." Why couldn't she recall going onto the bridge?

CHAPTER TWENTY

Ruth Okada

Tuesday afternoon, after looking for tile at three different stores, Ellen drove her friends to the excavation site on the Rose Garden plot at Rosario Cemetery to check on Bob's progress and to wait for the arrival of Ben Nishimura and Ruth Okada. However, Ben was already there standing over Bob and one of his students. The student was carefully using a brush to uncover another bone believed to belong to Haruto Okada. The rest of his skeleton lay on one of the four six-foot tables standing at the far corner of the tent.

"Still no sapphire?" Sue asked.

"No," Ben said. "But it's there. I know it is."

Ellen was beginning to wonder if there were more rumor than truth to the story Ben's grandfather had told him.

"What's wrong with your eyes?" Bob asked Ellen. "They're as red as watermelon wine."

"Dust at the fixer upper," she said. "I guess it got to me."

"Watermelon wine sounds delicious," Sue said. "Is it? I've never had it before."

"Well, then," Bob said with a laugh. "We'll have to do something about that."

"Promises, promises," Sue teased.

Ellen walked across the site to the table where the bones they believed belong to Haruto lay. She felt an overwhelming sadness as she thought about his young life—no older than Lane. Had Haruto's mother tucked him in at night? Had he gone to college after high school? She couldn't recall how old he was when he enlisted, but a voice inside her head told her that he was twenty-three and a college graduate. He'd taken a degree in business. She must have read that somewhere, she supposed.

She reached out and touched the top of the skull and shuddered with sadness.

"Please don't touch without gloves," one of the students beside her said.

Ellen hadn't even noticed the young woman. "Sorry."

At that moment another woman entered the tent. Ellen knew right away that it was Ruth Okada. She was a petite woman with white hair worn in a short bob, long lashes, and a round mole on her cheek. She wore readers on the top of her head, a red pantsuit, and black pumps. She carried a laptop bag strapped over her shoulder.

Somehow Ellen knew that Ruth looked a lot like her grandmother.

Before Ellen reached her, Ruth broke down into tears.

"It's like I can feel him," Ruth said. "It's such a strange feeling."

Ellen gave the woman a hug, to comfort her, but then her own tears began to fall again.

Pulling away, Ellen said, "I'm sorry it's taken you so long to find him."

"Where is he?" Ruth asked.

"Right here," Ellen said.

By that time, Ben, Bob, and Ellen's friends had crossed the tent to meet Ruth. Ellen introduced them.

"Here he is," Bob said as he led the group back to the tables. He pointed to the skeleton. "He was wearing dog tags with his name on it. We've already sent samples to our lab in Norman to analyze DNA. A sample from you would help us confirm his identity."

"Of course," Ruth said as tears slipped down her cheeks. "Oh, I wish my grandmother, Toshiko, were alive to see this. Hopefully she is watching down on us from heaven. Grandma, do you see? This is your husband, Haruto. Oh, dear God, please let her see."

Ellen burst into tears. "I'm sorry. I feel so emotional."

Ruth took her hand and squeezed it. "I can't thank you and your colleagues enough for this wonderful gift you have given me. How soon will you release his remains to me, so I can bury them with the rest of my family in Seattle?"

"Soon," Bob said. "As soon as we possibly can. I promise we won't keep him from you any longer than is necessary. We just want to make sure this really is your grandfather."

"I understand," Ruth said. "Thank you." Then she said, "In the email, you said you knew how he died."

"Maybe we should go someplace else, someplace comfortable, where you can sit down," Ben said.

"I just found him," Ruth said. "I'm not ready to leave him yet."

"He's not going anywhere," Bob said. "If you want to come back in an hour, I'll have more to show you."

"Can I see where you found him?" she asked.

"This way," Bob said.

Ellen and her friends followed Bob and Ruth across the lot on scraps of plywood to the unmarked grave where two students were carefully excavating the rest of Haruto's remains.

Ruth knelt on the dirt in her pretty pantsuit and touched the cool earth with her hands. Then she closed her eyes and moved her lips silently in prayer.

Ellen was overcome with emotion. She covered her mouth to stifle her sobs. Then Ruth picked something up in her hands.

"What's this? I think I've found a bone or something."

Bob thrust his hand into a glove and reached for it. "Let me have a look at it."

Ruth handed it over. Bob picked up one of the brushes from the planks of wood they'd laid around the site and brushed away the dirt.

"It's the sapphire," Ben said. "It belongs to Miss Okada."

"The what?" Ruth asked.

Ellen studied the stone that Bob was holding between his thumb and index finger. It was royal blue except for five white streaks that met at its center, forming a white star.

"I have a story to share with you, Miss Okada," Ben said as he took the sapphire from Bob.

"Please call me Ruth."

He helped her to her feet. She dusted the dirt from the knees of her pantsuit. Ellen felt a chemistry between them that reached beyond their ancestors.

"You have to eat dinner at some point," Ben said. "May I take you to my favorite restaurant and tell you my story?"

Ruth nodded as more tears spilled down her cheeks. "I'd like that. I've just arrived in town. Why don't I check in at the La Fonda, clean up a little, and meet you, say, around six?"

"I'm happy to drive you," Ben said. "If it's alright with you, I'll meet you in the lobby at six."

"Very good," Ruth said. "Thank you."

Although Ellen would have liked to have been invited, too, she could sense that Ben wanted to tell Ruth the story to her alone. She could understand not wanting a crowd to witness such a personal account of what had happened to her beloved grandfather.

"Why don't we go look at more tile?" Tanya whispered to Ellen.

"I need another hug," Ellen said to Ruth, holding open her arms.

"Of course," Ruth said.

Ellen held her close, feeling a kinship to the woman she couldn't explain. It was as if she were holding Alison after years of separation.

"I feel I know you," Ruth whispered. "You're a great comfort to me."

Ellen didn't want to let Ruth go, but she knew she had to. Pulling away, she said, "Let's talk more tomorrow, after Ben has shared his story. We have something we'd like to share as well."

"Of course," she said. "Until tomorrow."

Ruth kissed Ellen's cheek, filling her with warmth.

As Ellen and her friends were shopping for tile at one of the big warehouses Ricardo had recommended, Ellen got a call from Father Yamamoto.

"Hello, Father," she said into the phone.

"Hi, Ellen. I have a lead on who may have been responsible for vandalizing your garage door."

"Oh?"

"How soon can you meet me at the rectory?"

"We can be there in fifteen minutes," she said.

"See you then."

She ended the call and turned to her friends.

"What was that about?" Sue asked.

"Father Yamamoto has a lead on who vandalized my fixer upper," she said. "He wants us to meet him at the rectory."

"Let's go then," Tanya said. "But I think this tile is the winner, don't you?"

It was a classic arabesque pattern in antique linen. It looked gorgeous against the granite sample.

"Let's ask for one on the way out," Ellen said. "I want to know what Ricardo thinks before we put in the order."

Father Yamamoto was standing outside of the rectory watering a pot of flowering cactus when Ellen and her friends arrived.

"Your eyes are red," he said to Ellen without saying hello.

"The dust from my renovation irritated them earlier," she said dismissively.

"Well, come inside."

He opened the door for the three ladies and then followed them into the lobby.

"We're anxious to hear about this lead you have on the vandalism case," Sue said as she took a seat in the chair adjacent to the priest.

Ellen and Tanya sat on the couch opposite them.

"Where are my manners?" Father Yamamoto said. "Can I get you anything to drink?"

"No, thanks," Ellen said. "We're heading to dinner from here."

"You're welcome to join us," Tanya said.

"Thanks, but I have Teresa Castillo's rosary tonight. The funeral is tomorrow morning. Will you be attending?"

Tears rushed to Ellen's eyes at the memory of the young woman who'd so recently died. "I haven't decided yet."

"I think I'd like to go," Tanya said.

"Me, too," Sue said. "If it weren't for Teresa, we might not have solved this mystery."

"That brings me to why I called you over here," the priest continued. "Ever since our crossover ceremony at the bridge, people have been talking."

"What do you mean?" Sue asked. "Was it too much for them—knowing that their loved ones hadn't been at peace before now?"

"That's not what concerns me," he said. "Some—not all—are having trouble understanding the sympathy we feel for the Shinigami."

Ellen's stomach formed a knot.

"That's understandable," Tanya said. "Their loved ones were his victims."

"Father Martinez and I have discussed making forgiveness the focus of the upcoming weekend's masses, to help encourage these families to pray for the souls of those who have trespassed against them."

"That's always easier said than done," Sue said with a smirk.

"True," Father Yamamoto said. "It will take time, of course."

"You might also mention that as long as the Shinigami remains on this side, they're families are at risk," Sue pointed out.

"I'll mention that to Father Martinez," the priest said.

"I was hoping for a stronger lead regarding the vandalism," Ellen said.

"I can't tell you how I know this," Father Yamamoto began, "but I think it may have been one of Teresa Castillo's relatives. I'm not sure which one."

"Ellen is having surveillance cameras installed today," Sue said. "If they do it again, maybe we'll catch them, especially if we can narrow it down to one family."

"Ellen wouldn't press charges against a Castillo," Tanya said. "Would you, Ellen? So soon after Teresa's death?"

Ellen frowned, and, for a moment, she felt dizzy.

"Father Martinez has heard some confessions that concern him," the priest added. "Neither he nor I am at liberty to discuss what we hear in the confessional; however, it seems that our ceremony has stirred up quite a lot of Asian hate. He and I are worried that other crimes may follow. I just wanted to share this with you, so you understand why the vandalism has happened to you. People are hurt by what their loved ones suffered at the hands of the Shinigami. They were already upset by what happened to many of their ancestors during the Pacific War at the hands of the Japanese. Emotions are high, okay? You understand?"

Ellen nodded. "Thank you, Father. If you learn anything more, please share what you can without breaking any vows. I wouldn't mind catching the culprit and making them pay."

Father Yamamoto sighed. "So much for my lessons on forgiveness."

Tanya raised her brows at Ellen, but Ellen said nothing more about it.

Three hours later, as Ellen readied for bed in her hotel bathroom, she stared at her reflection in the mirror, noticing how red her eyes were.

That dust at the renovation site must have really gotten to her. She wondered if the shops downstairs were still open this late and if they carried eye drops. Then, since she was tired and already undressed, she decided she would check in the morning rather than make a trip down tonight. She brushed her teeth and then texted Brian before crawling into bed.

A moment later, he called her.

"Hello, you," she said into the phone.

He asked her how things were in Santa Fe. As she recounted the most recent events, tears flooded her eyes.

"It's just all so sad," she said. "An innocent girl is dead because of me."

"You can't blame yourself, Ellen," Brian insisted.

"But I do," she said as more tears spilled down her cheeks.

"Listen to me," Brian said.

"I need to go. I'll talk to you tomorrow."

Ellen ended the call and immediately received a text from Brian. He reassured her that she was not responsible and reminded her that he loved her. She put the phone on the nightstand, turned off the lamp, and tried to go to sleep.

But her mind was spinning.

I was once a good person.

"I *am* a good person," she said aloud. "I'm only trying to help."

I lost my humanity.

"What am I going on about?" Ellen said aloud. "Am I dreaming?"

I cared only for revenge until I saw things from your point of view.

"Haruto?" Ellen opened her eyes, switched on the lamp, and scanned the room for the shade with the red eyes, but she saw no one there.

I'm here. You know I am. You've known it all day.

Ellen sat up. "No. This is a dream."

How can you be dreaming if you are wide awake?

"This isn't happening." Ellen rushed to the bathroom, where she flipped on the light and stared at her reflection in the mirror. The red eyes of the shade of Santa Fe stared back at her from her own face.

In shock, she gaped and stared for a full minute. Her eyes were wide with terror even as they seemed to chide her in the glass.

"This can't be happening."

She touched her face with trembling fingers, still unable to believe that she wasn't alone. Nevertheless, she could feel him there, tethered to the back of her skull.

"Why are you doing this?" she asked with quivering lips.

I was going to kill you.

Her heart was beating fast. She took a deep breath and said, "Was?"

You may die yet. If the others discover our secret, they will try to save you. You may not survive.

"Haruto, please don't do this." Her knees gave out, and she clung to the vanity to support her weight.

All I want is a chance to speak with my granddaughter. I will leave you alone if you arrange it for me.

She grasped the *gris gris* bag hanging around her neck. She winced when she found it too hot to the touch. In the mirror, she noticed a rash on her chest where the bag had been pressed against her skin. She untied the leather cord and dropped the *gris gris* on the vanity.

Through chattering teeth, she asked, "What will happen to me? Can I survive this?"

Arrange a meeting with my granddaughter tomorrow, and I will leave you in peace.

Ellen raised a trembling hand to the mirror. She touched her hand to that of her reflection. "Why should I believe you? How do I know you aren't manipulating me?"

You'll have to take my word for it.

That's the last thing Ellen was capable of—trusting the word of a Shinigami. Feeling delirious, she resisted the urge to laugh.

"You're going to use me to take another victim. Is that it?"

I only want to see my granddaughter happy.

Ellen wished she could believe him. "You can't change that quickly. You've killed people for decades. That urge doesn't go away in the course of a single day."

Don't pretend you cannot feel my pain and remorse.

She sucked in her lips as more tears welled in her eyes.

It's my sadness that has produced so many tears for you today.

"Let my friends and I help you cross over to the other side," Ellen said as the truth of his remorse sank in.

I'm too afraid of what awaits me there.

"You're already in hell," Ellen reminded him. "The other side can't be worse than this. And there's a chance it will be better. Maybe you'll find peace."

No God would allow someone as evil as me into his kingdom.

"Father Yamamoto believes otherwise. And I believe in the goodness of humanity and in the redemption of the human spirit."

Those are nice things to believe in. Besides, I know what you really want. You want to get rid of me because you think I will take more victims.

Ellen placed her palms on the bathroom vanity and leaned toward the glass. "Wouldn't you like the chance to be reunited with Toshiko?"

Impossible.

"And not worth trying?" she challenged.

Ellen waited for the Shinigami's reply for several seconds before she realized that she had silenced him. A montage of his memories with Toshiko washed over her and calmed her nerves. They'd been a happy couple. He'd been so pleased by the pregnancy. He'd wanted nothing more than the opportunity to care for his family. That's why he had enlisted.

Ellen took advantage of the quiet in her head and climbed beneath the covers. She considered calling Sue and Tanya for help, but she was afraid that the Shinigami was right. If her friends attempted to exorcise him from her, it could kill her. Maybe if she gave him what he wanted, he would leave her voluntarily.

Maybe. Maybe not.

CHAPTER TWENTY-ONE

A Funeral

The Cathedral Basilica of St. Francis of Assisi was packed with people mourning for the passing of Teresa Castillo when Ellen and her friends entered the narthex. Ellen decided to leave her sunglasses on inside, because she was afraid that Father Yamamoto would recognize her Shinigami eyes. They had just found a seat near the back when the organ sounded throughout the church, and the procession moved up the aisle. An altar boy holding a tall crucifix led the procession. He was followed by two more carrying the wine and communion. Then Teresa's coffin, which was sitting on a base with wheels, was rolled up the aisle by six pall bearers, one of which was quite young—maybe seventeen. Finally, the priest, who must have been Father Martinez, brought up the rear. Ellen glanced around the church for Father Yamamoto and found him sitting in the back on the opposite side of the aisle from her. He gave her a half smile, which she returned as tears sprang to her eyes.

Throughout the mass, Ellen couldn't stop crying. When it was time to view the body, she followed Tanya and Sue up the aisle toward the altar, where the open casket was waiting. As she passed by pews full of people wearing solemn, grieving expressions, she felt their loss.

The guilt and remorse over what he had done overwhelmed him.

Haruto felt he did not deserve to be among these beautiful souls. He did not deserve to exist. He wished he could end his agony and disappear into oblivion. When he gazed upon the young woman's face whose life he had cruelly taken, he fell to his knees and wept.

Tanya turned back and extended a hand. "Are you okay?"

He took her hand and allowed her to help him back to his seat, but he wished he could fly away to a place where there was nothing, where he could feel nothing and think nothing.

For so long, he had taken comfort in his revenge. The one who had killed him, and those who had secretly buried him and left him abandoned and lost to his wife and family forever, would pay by watching their loved ones die. If Haruto couldn't be with his family, then his enemies could suffer with the loss of a few of their family members, too.

There was no lasting comfort in his revenge. It gave him but a moment of relief from his agony. Yet, he hadn't understood how evil he had become until he had possessed his most recent host.

She knew about him. She knew his name and how he had died. She also knew about his victims. Despite this knowledge, she wanted him to find his family and to find peace. Never in the many years since his death had he felt such profound love. And when he saw it reflected in the face of his granddaughter, Ruth, he was overcome with shame.

After the priest made his speech about eternal life in heaven, which Haruto had forfeited by allowing his vengeful heart to rule his existence for over half of a century, the father of Teresa Castillo stood behind the lectern to deliver a eulogy.

Haruto knew Armando Castillo. Haruto had tried to enter his body and lead him to the bridge, but Armando's soul had been too stoic to be led down a path of sadness and remorse. For many years, Haruto had revisited Armando, but the stoic soul could not be persuaded.

Standing now before his friends and family, Armando, an old man of sixty-five, no longer appeared stoic. His back was slouched, and his hands and lips were trembling. He did not gaze at the faces of his family and friends. He appeared a bent and broken man who could barely stand without the support of the lectern.

Without lifting his head, he said, "My daughter Teresa was a loving soul. As most of you know, she is survived by her mother, Angelina, and me, and by our son, Ray, and by our daughter, Juliana. She also has many loving aunts, uncles, and cousins, and beloved friends.

"Teresa had recently graduated from the University of New Mexico with a degree in journalism. Her dream was to become an investigative reporter. She was working at the bookstore until she could find the right job. She was so young. In many ways, she was just beginning her life.

"Her mother and I have spoken with Father Martinez, and we do not believe Teresa took her life willingly. As many of you know, she was interested in Suicide Bridge. She wrote about it on her blog. She interviewed many of you about those who took their lives there. And like other victims of Suicide Bridge, Teresa was not suicidal. She wasn't depressed. We believe she was possessed by an evil spirit, a devil who deserves to burn in hell. But we take comfort in knowing that she is with her Abuela in God's heavenly kingdom." Armando's voice faltered when he said, "We miss you, Teresa. We love you and miss you so much."

Haruto knew he would burn in hell if he crossed to the other side, and he wondered if he should face the music. But he was too afraid. He was a coward. He didn't want to suffer any more. He'd already suffered for far too long.

Then an idea came to him. Maybe there was a way he could stay on this side without being lonely, without suffering. Maybe there was a way he could even experience joy. He thought of his granddaughter, Ruth. Maybe there was a way they could spend eternity together.

Haruto wasn't sure how to detach himself from his host without killing her. He had made promises, but even as he had made them, he hadn't known if he could keep them. Each time he'd taken possession of a victim, his freedom came with their death.

Let me help you, Ellen's voice, dim and fading, said.

He couldn't believe she still wanted to help him. He had bared his soul to her—every ugly detail. It must be a trick. She wanted to trick him into going to the other side, where the devil was waiting for him.

No, she said. *Forgiveness waits.*

He smirked. He would not fall for her lies.

"After the funeral, we go to the bridge," he whispered to her. "It's the only way."

Her prayers filled his head, but he pushed them away and ignored them, just as he ignored her pleas to listen. When the service ended, he watched with renewed hope as the altar boys, pall bearers, and priest returned down the aisle to the music of the organ and the choir, ringing though the cathedral like a choir of angels. Tears filled his eyes—her eyes—as he waited for his turn to join the mourners down the aisle. He waited to leave the church, after which he would find a way to lead his victim to her death.

He didn't want to kill her. She was a loving soul who had understood him and who had wanted to help him. She and her friends had been responsible for bringing him and his granddaughter together, and for making it possible for his bones to be one day reunited with those of his beloved Toshiko and his son, Riku, whom he had never met.

He didn't want to kill his host, but he knew no other way to free himself from this body so he could possess his dear, kind Ruth and persuade her to spend eternity in his company. She had spent her life searching for him. It only seemed right that she should spend her death with him, never to be parted.

He had been so lonely, so very lonely for ages. Tears filled his eyes—her eyes.

Haruto had been so preoccupied with his plans, that he didn't notice that his host was plotting against him. Before he could stop her, Ellen threw herself into the fountain of holy water.

He screamed in pain and agony. The purity of the water burned. In a flurry of confusion and panic, he flew.

Ellen emerged from the water screaming. Her skin felt as if it had caught fire. She was hot and cold at once and shivered with fear and pain. A rush of people moved toward her, but Ellen was spinning, spinning, spinning, and then there was nothing.

Ellen awoke in a strange bed in a room she had never seen. Tanya and Sue were seated in small wooden chairs beside the bed. A crucifix hung on the wall over her head.

"Where am I?" she asked with a dry throat.

"Ellen, you're awake!" Tanya jumped to her feet and ran from the room. "Father Yamamoto, she's awake!"

Sue leaned forward. "You gave us quite a scare."

"I'm sorry." Ellen licked her dry lips. "Is there any water?"

Tanya, who had returned to the room, poured water from a pitcher into a glass before handing it to Ellen. Ellen struggled to sit up.

Father Yamamoto entered as Ellen drank from the glass.

"How do you feel?" he asked her.

"Tired but fine," she said. "How long have I been here?"

"Not quite an hour," Sue said. "Do you feel well enough to walk?"

Ellen sat up. "Okada, he…"

"We know," Father Yamamoto said. "I'm surprised that you weren't more seriously harmed when you jumped into the fountain."

"He wanted to leave me," she said as she slowly stood on her feet. "He wants to possess Ruth. We need to warn her."

"Why would he want to kill his own granddaughter?" Tanya asked.

"He doesn't want to cross over," she explained. "He thinks the devil will be waiting for him. He wants to stay, but he doesn't want to be alone."

"He wants to force Ruth to keep him company," the priest said with wide eyes. "We have to stop him. How soon can you arrange to be with Ruth?"

"She was hoping we'd meet her for lunch or dinner," Sue said. "I told her we'd have to see how you feel, Ellen."

"She doesn't know anything about the Shinigami," Tanya said.

"What time is it?" Ellen slipped her feet into her flats, which were on the floor near the bed.

"Half past one," Sue said.

"Call her and see if she can meet for a late lunch or an early dinner," Ellen said.

"Are you sure you're up for it?" Father Yamamoto asked.

She nodded. "Would you care to join us, Father?"

"Wednesdays are busy days for me. But text me if you need me. I'll keep my phone handy."

"Thanks for letting me rest here," Ellen said. "Is this your room?"

"A guest room," he said. "And you're more than welcome."

Sue climbed to her feet. "Ruth just replied that she and Ben are at El Farol on Canyon Road having tapas. She's invited us to join them."

"Are you sure you're up to it?" Tanya asked Ellen. "Your clothes are still damp, and your mascara is all over your face."

"Let's go. The sooner we explain all of this to Ruth and warn her, the better."

"Good," Sue said. "Because tapas sound delicious, and I'm starving."

"Me, too," Tanya said. "Thank you, Father."

"You ladies are always welcome," he said.

Ellen handed the rental key to Sue. "Can you drive so I can tidy myself on the way?"

"Of course," Sue said, taking the key.

When Ellen and her friends entered the restaurant, Ben Nishimura and Ruth Okada were standing together watching a waiter move their plates to a bigger table. Ellen thought Ben and Ruth looked like a nice couple.

"Oh, hello!" Ruth waved at Ellen, Tanya, and Sue.

Ellen waved back as she followed her friends through the restaurant to their table. Before sitting down, Ruth gave them each a hug. Ellen was relieved to see that Ruth's eyes weren't red.

"I'm so glad we finally have a chance to visit," Ruth said before taking her seat beside Ben. "Ellen, are you feeling better? Sue mentioned you weren't well earlier."

"I'm fine," she said, though she felt far from it.

"It smells good in here," Tanya said as she took her seat and picked up the menu. "I have no idea what to order."

Once they were all seated, Ben said, "For tapas, I recommend the Flash Fried Avocado with Pico de Gallo and Lime Crema. I also love the Brussels Sprouts with Bacon."

"I heard the steak was good," Sue said as she glanced over the menu.

"Everything on the menu is delicious," Ben said. "But you can get steak anywhere. That's why I recommend the tapas."

"Good point," Sue said.

After the waiter took their order, Ruth said, "I'm going to have to visit Santa Fe more often. Ben has been showing me around. He's been my personal tour guide. This city is quite fascinating, isn't it?"

"Is this your first time here?" Ellen asked.

"No, but it's been years."

"I took her to Meow Wolf this morning," Ben said with a smile. "We had an interesting time, didn't we?"

Ruth laughed. "We sure did."

"What about Santa Fe have you enjoyed the most, so far?" Sue asked.

Ruth glanced at Ben. "The people. The people are very friendly here."

Sue smiled and raised her brows at Ellen. She'd noticed the chemistry between Ruth and Ben, too. But Ellen found it hard to return Sue's smile. She was still worried about the Shinigami.

"Do you believe in ghosts, Ruth? Spirits and the hereafter? You know, things like that?" Ellen asked.

"Why, yes. My grandmother visits me in my dreams always asking the same question, 'Where is he?' Last night I could finally tell her that I found him." Tears welled in Ruth's eyes.

Ben patted Ruth on the back before taking another sip of his tea.

"The last few years of your grandfather's life were difficult, weren't they?" Ellen said. "Ben told you about Haruto's death, right?"

"I told her everything," Ben said.

"He thought I would blame him for something his grandfather did," Ruth said. "Well, that's just silly."

Ruth laughed and smiled warmly at Ben. He returned her smile.

"Have you ever heard of a Shinigami?" Sue asked Ruth.

"I've heard the legends and myths. Why?" Ruth glanced at each of the faces around the table and frowned.

"We believe that your grandfather became a vengeful spirit in the wake of his death," Ellen said. Then she told Ruth about Suicide Bridge and their theory that Haruto had possessed the descendants of Chuck Jensen, Rudy Castillo, Chayton Little, Jay West, Kiyoshi Nishimura, James Guerra, and Larry Thompson.

Ruth shook her head. "He wouldn't do such a thing. My grandmother told me he had a kind and loving heart. He wouldn't. He wasn't capable."

"Perhaps not while he was alive," Sue said. "But we change after death. We either cross over and rest in peace, or we wander the earth and lose our sense of humanity."

Tears slipped down Ruth's cheeks as she took everything in. "I don't know."

"Listen, Ruth," Ellen began. "He possessed me. I thought his thoughts and felt his feelings."

Ruth's mouth fell open and her brows disappeared beneath her white bangs. "What?"

"I think he was with me when I met you," Ellen said. "He was so happy to see you and so sad that it had taken such a long time. He was full of regret for what he had done. But he's afraid to cross over. He thinks the devil is waiting for him on the other side."

Ruth placed her hand on her heart. "How terrible. This can't be. Are you sure? How can you be sure? Couldn't you have imagined all of this?"

"Maybe we should dial this back a notch," Ben said. "This is a lot for her to process."

Ruth turned to Ben. "Do you believe it, too?"

"I didn't at first," he said.

Their conversation came to a halt when the waiters arrived with their tapas. After the waiters left, no one was in the mood to eat, even though the food looked and smelled delicious.

"I didn't at first," Ben repeated. "But they led a crossover ceremony at Suicide Bridge a couple of days before you arrived. I felt my daughter say goodbye. I don't know how to explain it." As he spoke, Ben's eyes filled with tears.

Ruth frowned. "And you believe my grandfather killed your daughter?"

Ben hesitated before saying, "I think it's possible."

"We hadn't planned on telling you this about your grandfather, Ruth," Ellen said. "But earlier today at the funeral of Teresa Castillo, well . . . ." Ellen shuddered, and her voice faltered.

"Ellen could hear Haruto's thoughts while he was in possession of her," Sue said. "Since he's afraid to cross over, he's decided to spend eternity here with you."

Ruth lifted her brows. "I'm okay with that. I already feel somewhat haunted by my grandmother. They can haunt me together."

Ellen shook her head. "You don't understand. He doesn't want to haunt you. Your grandmother doesn't haunt you. She visits you from the other side in your dreams. That's different. Haruto wants to kill you, so that your souls can be together."

Ruth gasped and stood up from the table. She looked down at everyone, her eyes blazing. "That's enough. I appreciate that you found him, but you're taking this way too far. No one can be sure when it comes to things like this. I don't want to hear any more about it. Excuse me while I use the ladies' room."

After Ruth left the table, Ellen apologized to Ben.

"We're just trying to help," Tanya said.

"I know," Ben reassured them. "Just give her time to process it all. It's a lot to take in."

"We need to protect her though," Ellen said. "We need to convince her to sleep in a circle of protection tonight and to avoid mirrors."

Suddenly, Ellen jumped to her feet. "Oh, no."

"Ellen? What's wrong?" Tanya asked.

"Mirrors. I think that's how he enters his victims."

Ellen rushed toward the ladies' room, hoping she wasn't too late. Tanya was on her heels. When Ellen opened the door to the bathroom, Ruth was at the sink washing her hands.

"Ruth?" Ellen asked.

Ruth turned and looked at Ellen with red eyes—Shinigami eyes.

CHAPTER TWENTY-TWO

A Trick with Treats

After Ruth left the ladies' room at El Farol Restaurant on Canyon Road, Tanya turned to Ellen. "What do we do?"

Ellen took her phone from her trouser pocket. "I'm calling Father Yamamoto."

Tanya nodded. "Okay. Gosh, I can't believe this is happening."

"Hi, Father, it's an emergency," Ellen said after the priest had answered.

"I thought as much. That's why I took the call. What's happened?"

"He's possessed Ruth. I can see him in her eyes. What should we do?"

"The only way to subdue him now is by giving her narcotics until we can perform an exorcism."

Ellen scoffed. "How am I supposed to do that?"

"Ply her with alcohol," he said. "Can you invite her to have drinks?"

"We're at a restaurant now. Do you think that will work?"

"It's your best chance of keeping the Shinigami from controlling her."

"Won't the alcohol make her weak and more susceptible to his manipulations?"

"If you give her enough to make her pass out, it will render her body useless to him."

Ellen clicked her tongue. "What if she refuses to drink that much?"

"Find a way to make it happen. Then get her to her room and tie her to the bed. I can meet you there this evening around seven o'clock. I'll ask Jane to join me."

"You want us to tie her to her bed?" Ellen gave Tanya a worried glance.

Tanya gazed back at her with wide eyes and whispered, "How are we supposed to do that?"

"If you can think of a better plan, go for it," he said.

"Okay, Father. I'll text you her room number. Pray for us."

"Always."

Ellen ended the call and immediately texted Sue and Ben the priest's instructions. Because two more women had entered the bathroom, Ellen showed the text to Tanya rather than risk being overheard.

Tanya read the text on Ellen's phone. "Oh my gosh, Ellen. I hope this works."

"Me, too," Ellen said. "Come on."

Ellen led Tanya back to the table where Ruth had taken her seat beside Ben. The look of worry on their faces made it obvious that Ben and Sue had received Ellen's text.

"How about a round of margaritas on me?" Ellen said as she returned to the table. "Get us off to a better start, okay?"

"I already beat you to it," Ben said with a smile. "Sue told me how the two of you like yours. Frozen, no salt, right?"

"Right," Tanya said. "Thanks."

"Hurry and taste your tapas," Sue said. "They're delicious. I'm nearly finished with mine."

"Aren't they amazing?" Ben said.

Tanya tasted hers, after which she said, "Mmm. They really are."

Ellen noticed that Ruth was frowning. "Ruth? You okay? I'm sorry about earlier. I shouldn't have shared my untested, unproven theory with you. Just pretend I never mentioned it."

"I know you're only trying to help, Ellen," Ruth said with tears in her red eyes. "The idea of it, though, has made me so sad. I can't shake it off."

Ellen gave Tanya and Sue a worried glance before saying, "Tell us more about your adventures with Ben in Santa Fe. Maybe that will cheer you up."

Ruth recounted their visits to galleries, museums, and shops, and her mood lifted as Ben joined her in their stories.

The waiter arrived with their margaritas. After he served them their drinks, Ellen said, "Go ahead and bring us another round, will you, please?"

"Yes, ma'am," the waiter said before leaving the table.

"That's nice of you, Ellen," Ruth began, "but I think one will be plenty for me. I'm not much of a drinker."

"Come on, Ruth," Ben said as he draped an arm across her shoulders. "We're celebrating. Remember?"

He raised his glass and said, "To your grandfather."

"To my grandfather," Ruth replied as she clinked the side of her glass to his.

"Cheers," Ellen and her friends said as they lifted their glasses, too.

"Mmm, that's good," Sue said of the margarita. "By the way, guys, while you were in the bathroom, Ben was telling me about the sapphire."

"Isn't he wonderful?" Ruth said, her red eyes gleaming. "He wants me to have it, but I refused. I told him we should sell it and split the proceeds."

"I told her I'd consider it if she went on a date with me," Ben said with a smile. "That's how I convinced her to spend the last two days with me."

"Oh, stop," Ruth said, grinning. "You know I would have said yes without the sapphire."

Ben leaned in and kissed her cheek. "Drink up."

Ellen was grateful for Ben's help, because she doubted that she and her friends could have encouraged Ruth to finish her margarita so quickly. By the time the waiter arrived with their second round, everyone's glass was empty.

"Cheers," Ellen said with her glass raised. "To the blue star sapphire."

"To the sapphire," Ben repeated.

They clinked glasses and drank.

Ellen ate her tapas, hoping to counter the effects of her margaritas. The alcohol was hitting her fast.

Although Sue had ordered a third round, Ruth had been unable to drink hers. Ellen could sense the worry from the others at the table. How would they manage to tie Ruth to her bed if they couldn't get her drunk enough?

Then she had an idea. She lifted her hand in the air and waved to the waiter. "Can I get tequila shots for the table?"

"What?" Ruth asked with her brows lifted. "No way."

"We're celebrating, remember?" Ben pointed out again.

She gave him a sheepish grin. "Are you trying to get me wasted, sir?"

He laughed. "Darn, she's on to me."

Ellen nodded to the waiter, and he left for their shots.

"We better call the shuttle to come pick us up," Tanya whispered to Ellen. "There's no way you're driving."

"You're right," Ellen agreed, giggling. "I haven't been this drunk in a long time."

When the tequila shots arrived, Sue lifted hers and said, "To Ruth's grandmother, for never giving up the search, and for instilling the same determination in her granddaughter."

"I'll drink to that!" Ruth said as she lifted her shot glass.

"Cheers!" they cried before they took their shots.

Ellen ordered another round of tequila shots and managed to suc-
ceed in getting Ruth to drink hers, but after that, Ruth flat out refused to
drink any more.

"I won't be able to walk," Ruth insisted.

Tanya whispered, "That's the point."

"Sshh," Ellen whispered back, worried that the drunken Tanya
would spill the beans.

"I'll call for the shuttle," Sue said with a stutter. Then, giggling, added, "My fingers are so slow!"

Ellen waved to their waiter and asked for the bill.

"Let me take care of it," Ben offered.

"Why don't we split it?" Ellen said. "Okie dokey?"

Ben laughed. "Well, when you put it that way…"

They settled their bill and made their way through the restaurant to
the exit, where they waited on benches for their shuttle.

"I'm so happy that you found my grandfather," Ruth said, "but so
sad that I never had the chance to meet him. My grandmother told me
so many stories. He liked to play jokes on her. Once he hid in the shower and, when she came to the bathroom, he scared her so bad that she
peed in her pants."

Sue laughed. "I think I may have just peed a little in mine!"

"Sue!" Tanya cried with a laugh. "There are people around."

"I don't care," Sue said. "At my age, I just don't care what people
think anymore. So what if I peed a little? Who cares?"

"Not me," Ben said with a laugh.

"There's our shuttle!" Ruth climbed to her feet. "Look! Isn't that it?"

"Yep, that's it," Ellen said, thinking it may as well be the ice cream
man, for all the excitement it was causing.

"Thank you so, so much!" Tanya told the driver as she boarded the
shuttle. "You're a real lifesaver!"

Ellen laughed at her usually quiet friend. "You tell him, girlfriend!"

They found their way to a seat. Ellen noticed that Ben had his arm around Ruth, and they were seated close together. Ellen lifted her brows and glanced at Sue and Tanya, who returned her grin.

A buzz near her hip made her take out her phone. It was a text from Ben: *She's invited me to her room. I'll text you when I've tied her up.*

Ellen frowned and replied: *But the Shinigami makes her strong—stronger than you. What if he tries to hurt you? Or kill you???*

She waited anxiously for his reply. When it finally came, she read: *If you don't hear from me in fifteen minutes, then come to the room.*

Ellen replied: *Okay, but please be careful.*

She showed the texts to Tanya, who was sitting beside her.

"Oh my gosh!" Tanya said, too loudly.

"What?" Sue wanted to know from the seat behind hers.

Ellen passed her phone back to Sue.

"I'm terrified!" Tanya squealed with a delirious grin.

"Sshh," Sue said, spitting all over herself and them.

The three friends giggled.

Ellen glanced across the aisle at Ruth, who was being kissed by Ben.

Good distraction technique, Ellen thought as she busted out laughing.

"Oh, no!" Tanya cried. "I'm going to be…"

Tanya threw up all over herself and Ellen.

The sight of it, along with the stench, made Ellen want to vomit, too. She jumped from her seat and cried, "Pull over, I'm going to be…"

She cupped her hand to her mouth and made her way to the front of the bus.

The driver stopped the shuttle, but before Ellen could hop out, she was sick all over the floor.

"I'm so sorry," she cried.

"They don't pay me enough for this," the driver murmured.

Ellen rifled through her purse for her wallet and pulled out a hundred-dollar bill. "For your trouble."

He took it but didn't seem pleased, so she gave him a second one.

"Thanks," he said. "Now take a seat, ma'am. We're nearly there."

Ellen glanced back to see that Sue was being sick in the aisle in back. The driver noticed in his rearview mirror.

Ellen grabbed another hundred from her purse and, while handing it to the driver, said, "Better out than in."

At the La Fonda, Ben and Ruth took a separate elevator, to avoid the smell.

"Goodbye," Ruth said to them. "I'll see you tomorrow at the cemetery?"

"Yes," Ellen said. "See you there."

Once Ruth and Ben's elevator closed and lifted to the next floor, Ellen pushed the elevator button again.

"I need a shower," Tanya said.

"We all do," Sue said. "But let's make it quick, ladies. Ben is in danger."

"They both are," Ellen said as the elevator door opened.

"What time is it?" Tanya wondered out loud.

"Oh, shoot. It's only five o'clock," Sue said. "Father Yama...wait, how do you say his name?"

"Yamamoto," Ellen said.

"He's not coming for two more hours," Sue said.

The elevator opened on their floor.

"We still need to hurry," Ellen said as she stepped into the hall. "Meet you here at the elevators in five minutes."

Ellen rushed into her room, showered off her body, and changed into fresh clothes. She didn't bother with hair and makeup. She brushed her teeth and was in front of the elevators in less than five. Tanya and Sue soon caught up to her.

"Have you heard from Ben?" Sue asked.

"He texted me her room number," Ellen said. "She's one floor up."

The elevator doors opened, so they stepped inside.

"You should ask him if he's okay," Tanya said, following.

"I did. He hasn't responded yet."

"Well, he could be busy," Sue said with a laugh.

"This isn't funny," Tanya said. "This is serious."

"It's a little bit funny," Sue insisted.

"I'm texting Father Yamamoto, to see if he can make it any earlier," Ellen said.

The elevator doors opened again, and they stepped out.

"This way," Ellen said, taking the lead.

When she reached the door of Ruth's hotel room, Ellen put her ear against it. She blushed as she heard a rhythmic pounding.

"I think they're having sex," she whispered. "I can hear the bed hitting the wall."

Tanya put her ear to the door. "How can we be sure? She could be beating him to a pulp."

"Let me listen." Sue pushed her way to the door and pressed one ear against it. "Hmm. It's hard to tell. It could be sex, or it could be murder."

Ellen made a fist. "I'm going to knock."

"Wait," Sue said. "He wanted fifteen minutes."

Tanya giggled. "Is that all he needs?"

"Stop," Ellen said, trying not to laugh. "This is serious, remember?"

Sue put her hands on her hips. "We should have bought her vodka instead of margs. Then we could have tricked her by drinking water and not be in such a hysterical state."

"It's too late now." Ellen glanced at the time on her phone. "I'm knocking in one minute."

They stood there quietly while Ellen watched the clock on her phone. After a minute had passed, she raised her fist to the door and knocked.

CHAPTER TWENTY-THREE

Exorcism

Ellen held her breath as she waited for someone to answer the door in Ruth's hotel room. She glanced nervously at her friends.

"Should I knock again?" she asked.

"You may as well," Sue said. "Maybe they didn't hear it."

Ellen knocked harder and was about to shout "Room service" when Ben opened the door. His shirt was off, his fly was open, and he was covered in sweat. There was a mark on his chest with blood dripping from it.

"You sure are fit," Ellen said without thinking. The alcohol was still affecting her.

"Did she bite you?" Sue asked.

"Come inside," Ben said as he opened the door wider and stepped back to make room for them to enter. "She's not very happy right now."

"Is that your fault?" Sue teased. "Sorry. Never mind me."

Ellen covered her mouth at the sight of Ruth lying flat on the bed beneath the covers with her arms tied behind her head.

"What's going on, Ellen?" Ruth cried. "Is this some kind of joke?"

"Calm down," Ellen said. "Everything's going to be okay."

"I'm not into anything kinky," Ruth insisted. "Please, Ben. Untie me."

"Is she naked beneath those covers?" Sue whispered to Ben.

"I'm afraid so," he said. "It was the only way I could…"

"You don't have to explain," Ellen said.

"Speak for yourself, Ellen," Sue said. "I would like to know what happened."

"Sue!" Tanya scolded.

"Please tell me what's going on," Ruth said again as she tugged against the socks that were holding her arms in place.

"She's not tethered to anything," Ellen whispered to Ben. "Father Yamamoto said to tie her to the bed."

"With what?" Ben asked. "It's not like I carry rope around."

"We need something strong," Tanya whispered. "Oh, we can use my belt."

"I tried that with mine," Ben said. "It wasn't long enough to get around the headboard."

"Connect them together," Sue said. "Here. Give them to me."

Sue buckled Ben and Tanya's belts together. Then she looped the belt around Ruth's wrists, pulled the belt through the buckle, and secured the end of the belt around the post of the headboard.

"Why are you doing this to me?" Ruth shouted. "What kind of twisted, sick game is this?"

"Stop yelling, or I'll put a sock in your mouth," Sue said sternly.

"Will that hold?" Tanya wanted to know.

"I don't know," Sue admitted. "Let's hope so."

Ruth made a strange snarling sound and with one yank, ripped the belt free of the headboard, though her arms were still bound by the socks. She lifted her arms and was about to sit up in the bed when Sue lay across her to hold her down.

Ellen covered her mouth and giggled deliriously.

As Ruth thrashed beneath Sue's weight, Sue cried, "Do something, fast!"

Following Sue's lead, Ellen lay across Ruth's legs. Then Ben held Ruth's feet still while Tanya took the belts and used them to tie Ruth's ankles together.

"That should slow him down," Tanya said. "But we need something else."

"The hair dryer," Sue said. "You can use the cord to tie her hands to the headboard more securely."

Ruth hissed, "Sickos!"

Tanya scrambled to the bathroom and returned with the hair dryer. Ben took it and used the cord to make a better bind around the post of the headboard.

All the while, Ruth snarled and growled, her eyes even redder than they were before.

Sue climbed to her feet. "I'm calling Jane."

"I'll call Father Yamamoto," Ellen said.

When the priest didn't answer, she texted him Ruth's room number along with 9-1-1.

Then Ellen said, "Haruto, please let us help you."

In a voice that sounded low and gravelly and nothing like Ruth's voice, Ruth said, "Why should I trust someone who has trapped me twice?"

"We couldn't let you kill your granddaughter," Sue said. "You would have regretted it, anyway. She would have resented you for cutting her life short just as she's finally found love."

Ellen glanced at Ben, who blushed.

"You should clean that wound," Tanya said to Ben.

"I'm fine," he said. "I'm more worried about her."

Tanya got up and went to the bathroom and returned a moment later with a wet washcloth. She gave it to Ben, and he used it to wipe the blood from his upper chest, where he appeared to have been bitten.

"Jane just texted that she's on her way," Sue said.

"Thank goodness," Tanya said.

Ruth hissed. "Unbind me, or I'll kill her now!"

"Don't you dare, you asshole!" Ben said angrily.

Ellen raised her hands to Ben, motioning for him to calm down. Then to Ruth, she said, "Don't do anything rash, Haruto. Listen to me. Your granddaughter loves you now. She loves you so much. But if you kill her, she'll hate you for it. And how do you think your wife will feel about it? Huh? Toshiko raised Ruth. Ruth is like a daughter to her. She would never forgive you if you took Ruth's life."

Tears fell from Ruth's red eyes.

Sue said, "She's waiting for you on the other side, Haruto. Leave Ruth alone and go to your loving wife before you do something you'll regret more than anything you've done before."

Ruth fell quiet and stared at the ceiling as tears ran from the corners of her eyes.

They were quiet for several minutes until there was a knock at the door.

"That must be Jane," Sue said.

"I'll get it," Ben offered.

When Jane entered, Ellen caught her up with what had happened so far.

"We need to get everything ready," Jane said. "Help me with the incense burner."

Jane had a silver censer that hung on a chain. It was like the one Father Yamamoto had used at the crossover ceremony.

"We need to bathe everyone with the smoke," Jane said.

Once the censer was smoking, Jane walked with it around the room, helping the smoke to wash over each of them, including herself. Then she turned to Ruth and said, "My dear, this may hurt, so brace yourself."

"Stay away from me!" Ruth said in a voice that was not her own.

Jane ignored the comment and held the censer over Ruth's body with one hand while she waved the smoke over her with the other.

Ruth screamed.

"I meant what I said about the sock," Sue said. "Should I stuff it into her mouth?"

Ruth fell silent and began to weep again. She writhed for a moment, and then, in her own voice, she said, "He's gone. He left me. You can let me go now."

But Ruth's eyes were still red. Haruto was trying to trick them.

When Jane had finished bathing Ruth with the smoke, she set the censer on the table and reached into her bag, pulling out three candles. "Help me light these."

Sue found a lighter in her purse and helped Tanya to station the candles in a circle on the table.

"Father Yamamoto just texted that he's on his way," Ellen said. "Oh, thank God!"

Ruth hissed.

"Listen to me, Haruto," Ellen said. "Toshiko is waiting for you on the other side. You have to believe me."

"She speaks the truth," Jane said. "I'm calling on all of God's angels and saints and on your wife Toshiko and your son."

"Riku," Ellen said. "He's waiting for you, too."

More tears spilled down Ruth's cheeks.

"The devil waits for me," Ruth said.

"Let's say the Lord's Prayer," Jane suggested. Then she began, "Our Father, who art in heaven…"

Ellen, Sue, Tanya, and Ben joined in the prayer. Ruth continued to weep.

Just as the prayer came to an end, Ellen went down on her knees beside the bed and touched Ruth's cheek. "Please, Haruto. I know that, deep down, you're a good man. I thought your thoughts and felt your feelings. I know you want to do the right thing. Let your granddaughter live. Join your loved ones on the other side."

There was another knock on the door.

"It's the priest," Tanya said from where she was looking through the peephole.

She opened the door, and Father Yamamoto rushed inside. He was wearing his purple stole.

"Please tell me I'm not too late," he said.

"Ruth's still alive," Jane assured him. "And Ellen seems to be connecting with Haruto. I think we should let her take the lead."

Ellen looked at them in surprise. "Me?"

"You have bonded with him. I can sense he's listening to you," Jane said.

"Tell me what to do," Ellen said.

"Keep him calm," Father Yamamoto instructed. "What you're doing seems to be working. Just be on guard against him trying to re-enter you."

The priest took his holy water sprinkler from his bag and shook it over everyone in the room. Ruth hissed with pain when the drops touched her skin. Ellen caressed her cheek.

"It's okay," Ellen said. "You're going to be okay."

"Continue to reassure him while I say a prayer," Father Yamamoto said.

Ellen did as the priest said. She was trembling because now she was worried that Haruto might possess her again, and maybe this time, she wouldn't survive it.

"God, whose nature is ever merciful and forgiving," the priest began with his palms raised, "accept our prayer that this servant of yours, bound by the fetters of sin, may be pardoned by your loving kindness. Please accept Haruto Okada into your heavenly kingdom. Please ask your heavenly angels and saints to welcome him with open arms."

Ruth began to weep again.

"It's okay," Ellen whispered. "You are loved. No matter what you've done, God's love is unconditional."

"God, our Father, I implore you to take your servant, Haruto Okada. Pull his spirit from the body of his granddaughter, Ruth Okada. Welcome him home while sparing the life of his precious host."

Ruth abruptly widened her eyes, and her body jerked into a straight line.

"Ruth?" Ellen asked as she sat back on her heels. "Are you okay?"

"I see them on the other side," Jane said with a smile on her face. "Do you see them, Father?"

"Yes, I do! They're so beautiful!"

"What do you see?" Sue asked.

"Haruto's victims," the priest said. "They're welcoming him to heaven. They've forgiven him."

"What?" Ellen couldn't believe that the victims of Suicide Bridge could so easily forgive their killer. Some for them had suffered for decades.

"I wish I could see," Tanya whispered.

"Don't look with your eyes," Jane said. "Look with your mind's eye."

"How do I do that?" Tanya asked.

"Try closing your eyes," Jane suggested.

Ellen closed her eyes and reached out with what she hoped was her mind's eye. From behind her lids, she saw nothing but darkness. She willed herself to see the victims of Suicide Bridge. She was especially anxious to see Teresa Castillo. She wanted to know that she was happy.

"I see them!" Ruth cried. "I can't believe they don't despise me!"

"I see them, too!" Tanya said.

"I don't see anything," Sue said. "And I'm the one with the gift."

Ellen opened her eyes and glanced around the room. Jane and Father Yamamoto were looking toward the ceiling. Sue and Tanya's eyes were tightly shut. Ruth's eyes were wide open. So was her mouth, though its corners were stretched in a way that Ellen couldn't tell was a smile or a grimace. Perhaps it was both.

"God, our Father, please accept Haruto Okada into your heavenly kingdom," Father Yamamoto prayed. "Please forgive him his trespasses as we have. Show him your loving mercy and generous spirit. Welcome him into your family of angels."

Suddenly, Ruth shrieked, and her entire body convulsed. That's when Ellen saw him—not with her eyes, but with her mind's eye. She recognized him from Meow Wolf and from the other times he had appeared to her. Now, as he floated toward the ceiling, he smiled down at her.

"Thank you," he mouthed, though no sound came from his lips.

Tears sprang to Ellen's eyes as she covered her mouth. Just as Haruto reached the ceiling, Ellen saw the others waiting for him. She gasped at the sight of their smiling, loving faces and the warm expressions they wore. Teresa Castillo was among them.

Then the old woman from Ellen's dreams held her arms open to Haruto. As he kissed her cheek, her appearance changed to that of a young woman in her twenties. Haruto kissed her again and held her in a tight embrace.

"Do you see that?" Ellen whispered to the others.

"Yes," Tanya said with her eyes closed. "It's a miracle."

"What do you see?" Sue asked.

"I see Jenna," Ben, whose eyes were open and filled with tears, said.

Tanya leaned over Ellen to touch Ruth's shoulder. Ruth's eyes were closed, and her body was listless.

"Ruth?" Tanya asked. "Are you okay?"

The woman didn't move.

Ben rushed to her side and untied her wrists. "Ruth? Can you hear me?"

Ruth opened her eyes. Ellen was relieved that they were no longer red.

"I need water," Ruth said.

Ben found a water bottle in the minifridge, opened it, and gave it to her.

"Am I the only one who didn't see what happened?" Sue asked.

"Maybe you were trying too hard," Jane said. "Sometimes, you have to let go of yourself. Only then can you see."

"It was incredible," Tanya said, her eyes still moist with tears.

Sue put her hands on her hips. "Don't rub it in, Tanya."

"Maybe we should go and let Ruth get some rest," Father Yamamoto said.

"That's not a bad idea, Father," Ben agreed.

Ellen climbed to her feet from where she had been kneeling beside the bed. "I think I'm ready to try some of Tanya's lavender tea. My nerves are still rattled."

"What happened?" Ruth asked. "Why are all of you here?"

"I thought you were having a heart attack," Ben said quickly as he glanced around at the others. "They came to help."

Ruth pulled the covers to her neck. "How embarrassing."

"What's the last thing you remember?" Sue asked.

Ruth rubbed her eyes. "I think it was the second tequila shot."

Sue turned to Ben. "I guess you didn't make much of an impression."

Jane's jaw dropped open, and Father Yamamoto pretended not to have heard.

"Sue!" Tanya scolded as Ben's face turned darker than a turnip.

"It was a joke!" Sue insisted. "Golly!"

"We'll see you at the cemetery in the morning," Ellen said as she ushered her friends from the room. Then she turned to Tanya. "I'm serious about that tea. You got any?"

"I sure do. Come to my room and I'll make us some."

CHAPTER TWENTY-FOUR

Homecomings

Thursday morning, Ellen, Sue, and Tanya met downstairs in the restaurant of La Fonda for their usual breakfast, except, this time, Tanya brought lavender tea bags. Sue and Ellen had noticed that drinking hot lavender tea had made them feel less anxious about everything that had happened in Santa Fe.

As they waited for their order, Sue said, "I think I'll have some of this tea before my procedure next week."

"What procedure?" Ellen asked.

"Remember? I'm finally getting my IUD removed."

"It's about time," Tanya said. "You've been post-menopausal for a year now, haven't you?"

"I know, I know. I don't need a lecture. I've been scared. I've heard stories that it can get embedded if left for too long."

"I'm sure you'll be fine," Ellen said.

"Well, I don't know about that," Sue said. "The speculum is always enough to give me bad cramping. My doctor says that's unusual."

"I was just going to say that I never feel anything," Tanya said. "Did your doctor explain why it hurts you?"

"Apparently I'm as tight as a virgin," Sue said with a grin before singing Madonna's, "Like a virgin, touched for the very first time." Then she said, "Tom's a lucky man."

"Sue!" Tanya chastised. "That's too much information!"

Ellen shook her head and rolled her eyes.

After their food had arrived, Ellen felt her phone buzzing, so she took it from her purse and found a text from Father Yamamoto.

"Oh, listen to this," she said to her friends. "Father Martinez spoke to Armando Castillo, Teresa's father, this morning. Armando told him about an interesting dream he had last night. A young Japanese man appeared to him, begging to be forgiven for taking the life of Teresa. At first, Armando refused. But then his daughter appeared in the dream, too, and pleaded with her father on Haruto's behalf, saying that to deny forgiveness would only trouble Armando in the future. Armando finally agreed. Father Martinez told this story to Father Yamamoto, and he wanted to pass it on to us. Isn't that wonderful?"

"It truly is," Tanya said.

"I still don't think it was right that I couldn't see anything last night," Sue said. "Maybe I'm losing my mojo."

"You aren't losing your mojo," Ellen assured her. "It was probably the alcohol. If you'd been less drunk, then maybe you would have seen."

"I bet you're right," Sue said, perking up. "Though I don't think it's enough of a deterrence to prevent me from having more margaritas."

Ellen and Tanya chuckled.

An hour later, the ladies took the rental to the tent site. When they arrived, Ben and Ruth were already there talking with Bob. His students were huddled on the ground in various spots throughout the plot carefully excavating more remains.

"Oh, hello!" Ruth cried when Ellen and her friends entered the tent from the opposite side. "Dr. Brooks has good news."

Ellen followed Tanya across the site on the scrap plywood to where Ruth and the others were gathered near the tables with the bones.

"Good morning," Bob said.

"Hey, Bob," Sue said. "What's up?"

"My lab confirmed a DNA match between Miss Okada and the remains we found with the dog tags," he said.

"That's wonderful news," Ellen said. "And fast."

"I called in a favor," Bob explained.

"I can't thank you all enough for what you've done," Ruth said. "This means so much to me and to my grandmother. I plan to have a memorial in Seattle in two weeks. You are all invited. I'll text and email you the details."

"Thank you," Sue said.

"How nice," Tanya added.

"I would very much like to be there," Ben said with a smile.

"Me, too," Ellen said glancing at her friends, who nodded their agreement.

Then Sue leaned closer to Ruth and asked, "Can you really not recall anything that happened after our second shot of tequila?" Sue lifted her brows in Ben's direction.

Ruth's face turned as red as a fire engine.

Ellen took Sue by the arm and said to Ruth, "We need to go and check on the renovation. Have a safe flight back to Seattle!"

As they headed to their rental, Tanya said, "Really, Sue! How embarrassing!"

"Sorry, ladies, but inquiring minds want to know."

When they arrived at the house on Luna Circle, Ellen was disappointed to learn that the vandal had returned. Ricardo, who had already covered the words with paint, believed it had happened sometime the previous night.

"I'll find out soon enough," Ellen said as she grabbed her phone from her purse. "We can watch the footage on the home security website. I just need to log in."

Her friends waited beside her with Ricardo in the driveaway as Ellen logged in and searched through the camera footage.

"It's a kid," Ellen said. "A girl I think."

"Let me see," Sue insisted, taking the phone from Ellen. "That's Julianna Castillo."

"You aren't going to press charges, are you, Ellen?" Tanya asked. "She's just upset over losing her big sister."

"Of course not," Ellen said. "That was Haruto's anger driving me the other day when I said otherwise."

"How scary," Tanya said.

"Maybe we could ask Father Yamamoto to ask Father Martinez to say something to Julianna about forgiveness."

"That's a good idea," Ellen said. Then she turned to Ricardo. "Sorry to keep you waiting. How's the renovation coming along?"

"Very well, ma'am," he said. "Come and have a look at your kitchen."

Ellen and her friends followed Ricardo inside, where the cabinets and granite countertops had already been installed and the backsplash was in progress. The walls had been painted as well, bringing all the colors together beautifully.

"Oh, Ellen," Tanya said enviously. "This looks amazing."

"I agree," Ellen said. "Well done, Ricardo."

"Thank you, ma'am," he said. "The fixtures came in today. He lifted one from an opened box on the floor. "Aren't they beautiful?"

The copper pendants were breathtaking against the granite.

"Wow," Sue said. "Copper was definitely the right choice."

"And once we install the honey oak floors, it will look even better," Ricardo said. "They should arrive in the next day or two, and we'll begin installation at the end of the week—after the wood has had a chance to acclimate."

Ellen clapped her hands with excitement. "I can't wait."

"How far down do you want these pendants to hang over the peninsula?" Ricardo asked as he held one of them over the countertop. "I would recommend about here. What do you think?"

"Perfect," Ellen agreed. "Just so you know, we're driving back to San Antonio in the morning, but you can call or text me with any other questions."

"Sure, no problem," he said. "When will you be back to Santa Fe?"

"Whenever the job is complete," she said. "In about five weeks?"

"Yes, ma'am," Ricardo said. "You can count on it."

Ellen traced her hand along the smooth granite, reminiscent of Van Gogh's *Stormy Night*, and sighed. Her trip to Santa Fe had been like a stormy night, and like Van Gogh, she and her friends had managed to make something beautiful out of it. She was proud.

Turning to Sue and Tanya, she said, "We need to reunite Ghost Healers, ladies. Our work is too important to neglect. Think of all the good we might still do."

"I was thinking the same thing," Sue said. "In fact, I planned to have you convinced by the time we reached San Antonio."

They turned to Tanya.

"You don't have to convince me. I'm in!"

It was after five o'clock on Saturday when Ellen finally arrived home after dropping Tanya and Sue at their respective houses. She still had the rental and would have Brian follow her to return it in the morning. Right now, she just wanted to be home.

When she pulled into the drive, she noticed Nolan and Lane's cars parked on the curb. Had her children come to see her?

Without getting her luggage from the trunk, she rushed inside. Brian and her kids, along Nolan's wife Taylor and Lane's girlfriend Maya, were seated around the dining room table.

"There she is!" Brian said as he got up from his chair. "Welcome home, darlin'."

He gave her a kiss on the cheek. Then she rushed around and received hugs from Nolan, Taylor, Alison, Lane, and Maya.

"What a wonderful surprise," Ellen said. "Excuse my appearance. I must look awful."

"You're beautiful, as always," Brian assured her.

She draped her purse over the back of her chair before taking a seat. "What's the occasion?"

"Lane said he has some news for us," Nolan said. "He wouldn't tell us without you."

Ellen glanced from Lane to Maya, noticing their bright smiles and gleaming eyes.

"Are you two pregnant?" Ellen asked.

Lane scoffed. "No, Mom. We're engaged. We're going to get married."

Ellen jumped to her feet. "Oh, how wonderful! I'm so happy for you! Welcome, to the family, Maya!"

She hugged each of them again. "Sorry about the pregnancy comment. I just can't wait to have more grandchildren."

"That's okay," Maya said with a laugh. "We'll try to accommodate you as soon as possible."

Taylor cupped her baby bump. "It won't be long now."

Ellen kissed Taylor's cheek. "I'm so excited."

Brian raised his glass of wine. "Congratulations! A toast!"

Nolan and Alison jumped to their feet and fist bumped their brother before picking up their glasses of wine and joining in for a toast.

Brian handed Ellen a glass, and she said, "Cheers!" before taking a sip and returning to her seat.

After their toast, Maya showed them all the ring. "Lane picked it out and surprised me."

"It's beautiful!" Alison said. "When did he propose?"

"It happened over a month ago," Lane said, "but we were waiting on Mom. We've already set the date and everything."

"Really?" Nolan asked. "So, when's the big day?"

Maya glanced nervously at Lane before saying, "I hope you won't hate this idea."

"Why? When is it?" Alison asked.

"Christmas Eve," Lane said. "At the Biltmore Estate in Asheville, North Carolina."

"Are you okay with that?" Maya asked them. "It may not be the way you planned to spend Christmas."

"I love it," Ellen said. "As long as we're together, I don't care where we are. And the Biltmore? I hear it's beautiful at Christmastime."

"It really is," Maya said. "It's been my mother's dream to have my wedding there since I was a little girl."

"We're happy to help however we can," Brian said. "Don't hesitate to ask."

"Please invite your brother and his family," Lane said to Brian.

"I'm sure they'd love to come," Brian said.

Lane turned to Ellen. "Do you think Uncle Jody and his family can make it? And Uncle Gordon and Aunt Lou Cinda?"

"I'll make sure of it," Ellen said. "Do you mind if I include Tanya and Sue and their families?"

"The more the merrier," Maya said.

Ellen squeezed Brian's hand and glanced around the table at her family, trying to soak in all the joy.

"Your father would have been so proud," Ellen said to Lane. "I'm sure he's smiling down at us right now."

"I wish he could have been here for this," Lane said as he wiped away a tear.

"He will be there, honey," Ellen said as she squeezed Brian's hand again. "I'm sure of it."

Two weeks later, Ellen and her friends and their spouses flew together to Seattle for Haruto Okada's memorial. Ellen had finally come clean and had told Brian everything that had happened in Santa Fe, including her and Ruth's possessions. She'd been surprised that he hadn't chastised her for risking her life. He showed nothing but pride and admiration in her risk-taking for the good of other souls. She was relieved and pleased and vowed to never keep anything from him again. But she warned him not to talk about it on the plane, because Sue and Tanya hadn't been as forthcoming with their husbands.

The ceremony was lovely, and Ellen was happy to finally see Haruto's remains reunited with those of his wife and son. It was a simple ceremony with a small group in attendance. Ruth had no other family members, but she belonged to a book club, and eight of its members showed up along with a few of her coworkers. Ben Nishimura was there, of course, but Bob had been unable to come. After the ceremony at the graveside, the group went to a restaurant to share a meal.

During their conversation over lunch, Ruth revealed that Ben was moving to Seattle to live with her. He said that he could make art anywhere, and he hated being separated from her. Ellen wondered if a wedding was in their future.

Three weeks later, Ellen and her friends and their spouses took another flight together—this time to Santa Fe, to see the house on Luna Circle. Ricardo was there to greet them at the front door.

"Tom, this is Ricardo," Sue said with a grin.

"So, you're the one she can't stop talking about," Tom teased.

Ricardo blushed.

"I told him that you are very talented with interior design," Sue said defensively.

"That's not all she said," Tom said with a laugh.

Ricardo led them inside. The first thing Ellen noticed was the beautiful and rich honey oak floors. They were gorgeous.

But then her eyes didn't know where to look next. The furniture Ricardo had helped her to pick out online looked stunning, along with the other décor. The rooms looked better than anything she'd seen on HGTV or in a magazine.

Ellen told the husbands about how it all began with the granite. She talked about the light and airy vibe they were going for. She showed them her workspace near the back windows, where Ricardo had set up an easel and small artist table.

"Let me show you *our* room," Sue said to Tom.

Tanya glanced at Ellen and rolled her eyes before saying, "Our room is better, Dave."

"Let's see the master," Brian said to Ellen.

As she led him from the kitchen, she noticed a gift bag on the dining table. "Oh, Sue, look at this. Bob Brooks sent us a bottle of watermelon wine."

Sue stepped back into view and said, "Wasn't that nice? I like it when a man keeps his promises." Then, turning to Tom, she said, "He's just another one of my admirers. But you have nothing to worry about."

"I want to see the bridge," Brian said.

Sue visited with Ricardo on the back patio while the others made the trek up the hill to the ravine and Suicide Bridge.

"We need to think of a new name for it," Ellen said.

"Why not Ellen's Bridge," Brian said. "It's your retreat."

Ellen shook her head. "I want to call it something meaningful."

"We wouldn't have solved the mystery without Teresa Castillo," Tanya pointed out. "Why don't you name it after her?"

"I love that," Ellen said. "From now on, it's the Teresa Castillo Bridge."

"You should write to her family," Tom said. "I bet they'd like that."

"I will," Ellen said. "Good idea."

"Now where are these tapas you ladies have been talking about?" Dave wanted to know.

After a fabulous weekend of shopping and tapas, the three couples flew back to San Antonio.

On the plane where they sat together in first class, Ellen reminded her friends about Lane's wedding on Christmas Eve.

"I really hope you and your families can make it. Have you had a chance to check with them?" Ellen asked.

"I don't care if they can make it," Sue said. "Tom and I will be there. Won't we, Tom?"

"Do I have a choice?" he asked from across the aisle.

"It's the largest privately owned home in the nation," Dave said, "built in the style of the French chateau. It's as big as a frickin' castle. I'm looking forward to it. Who cares about the kids?"

"Dave!" Tanya chastised. "He doesn't mean that. And the kids have already said they can make it."

"Oh, good," Ellen said. "Because it wouldn't be the same without my besties there."

Sue lifted her brows. "Ellen and Tanya, y'all do know that the Biltmore is haunted."

"Really?" Ellen said. "I didn't know that."

"Maybe we should take our gear, just in case," Tanya said with a smile.

"Look at you, Tanya," Sue said. "We'll have to call her the brave one from now on."

Tanya crossed her arms. "I've always been the brave one. The bravest people are those who have the greatest fear but persevere anyway."

"That's true," Ellen said. "Alrighty, then. Biltmore ghosts, here we come."

THE END

Thank you for reading my story. I hope you enjoyed it! If you did, please consider leaving a review. Reviews help other readers to discover my books, which helps me.

Please visit my website at evapohler.com to get the next book, *A Holiday Haunting at the Biltmore.*

EVA POHLER

Eva Pohler is a *USA Today* bestselling author of over thirty novels in multiple genres, including mysteries, thrillers, and young adult paranormal romance based on Greek mythology. Her books have been described as "addictive" and "sure to thrill"—*Kirkus Reviews*.

To learn more about Eva and her books, and to sign up to hear about new releases, and sales, please visit her website at https://www.evapohler.com.

CPSIA information can be obtained
at www.ICGtesting.com
Printed in the USA
BVHW060209130123
656254BV00011B/349